REGAN

REGAN

IAN KENNEDY MARTIN

HOLT, RINEHART AND WINSTON | NEW YORK

M

Library of Congress Cataloging in Publication Data
Martin, Ian Kennedy.
Regan.
I. Title.
PZ4.M38116Re3   [PR6063.A715]   823'.9'14   75–940
ISBN 0–03–014541–4

Designer: Victoria Gomez

Printed in the United States of America

Patrolman Dennis O'Hagen sat in a field bordering the town of Anselmo (population 1,480), Northern California, for two days and nights and nobody seemed to notice him. Presumably even for a small town like Anselmo there'd be some crimes through those forty-eight hours; like it was known Mrs Kleimber was screwing a school kid, male, under age, and Mr Neil Bean was stealing money off his wife, which was a crime. And there was in fact an automobile collision which O'Hagen's eyes must have witnessed—and Mr Levitt was in the wrong for sure, and not Mr Thomson which it looked like, him coming out of a side street on to the main drag. But Patrolman O'Hagen, although no doubt registering all this, was not doing anything about it. O'Hagen was sitting upright against a tree in the middle of some bushes. There was a small hole between his staring eyes. It had been caused by a 9-millimetre Walther automatic. The shot that killed him had been fired from very close range.

The boy scout who found him was near eleven and cool. He felt for the man's pulse, touched nothing else, and ran high speed to Mrs Carey's place which was nearest.

As it was the murder of a policeman they sent 21-Unit out of Frisco—five large detectives, none of them friendly with the natives of Anselmo who would have liked to have been helpful. As it happened the murder had nothing to do with the town. When the five detectives reconstructed the last moments of O'Hagen's life, it went like this.

1

He was on patrol on the main road into Anselmo. Some automobile passes, maybe speeding. O'Hagen overtakes the guy, presumably waves him down, the man hesitates, the two cars stop with a minor collision. The guy's car bangs into the back of O'Hagen's car. He then shoots the cop and sticks him in the bushes with a view over the town. He goes back to his car, and makes one mistake.

In the collision the two cars must have linked fenders, the killer's front fender on top of the cop's rear fender. The murderer must have gripped his own fender, done some weight lifting and got his automobile free. However, he left one thumbprint and a smudged index fingerprint on the rear fender of the cop car.

O'Hagen's car was carefully examined for fingerprints, including the area which showed collision damage. The police mechanic, Maltby, was pretty sure that on the day of the cop's death, when he went out on patrol, that car was undamaged. Within hours, 21-Unit out of Frisco had a suspect. The prints on the fender belonged to a James Purcell, alias Eddie Christopher, alias Hunt Kalman, etcetera. 21-Unit reckoned a guy who had knocked off a cop was in a hurry to move towns. They checked the airports. A man called James Purcell, answering the description of the wanted man, took the Pan Am polar flight, San Francisco–Los Angeles–London, twenty-four hours previously. It was a one-way ticket. But it had been booked a month before.

21-Unit, San Francisco Police, followed the recognized procedure, which was to inform the Federal Bureau of Investigation who then telexed a wire photo and all details to New Scotland Yard, that a cop-killer was in London.

About a hundred miles from London, in Stroud, in the Cotswold area, a reasonably well-known criminal called Eddie Mavor pulled up at the traffic lights alongside a Daimler Van Den Plas limousine. The Daimler had smoked glass side and rear windows, like a pop star's car. The driver's compartment—it had a chauffeur's division—was plain glass all round.

Eddie Mavor was driving a Jensen Interceptor, his pride and joy. There were two joys in his life, a girl called Shirleen, eighteen, a stripper whom he employed and laid at the London night-club he owned, and the Jensen Interceptor. If he ever had to make the choice between loves, the lay would go.

At the traffic lights he looked idly across at the chauffeur of the Daimler. The chauffeur was studying him. Mavor's eyes wandered off for a moment taking in the main street of the pretty town, the grey Cotswold stone buildings under a weak sun. Spring daffodils lined up like parading troopers in the Norman churchyard.

The main street deserted. Two cats sunning themselves without real sun. Lunch hour. Not one single human in sight.

Mavor looked back at the chauffeur and did a double-take. The traffic lights were still at red. The chauffeur had raised the thumb on his right hand and was looking directly at Mavor. In any language that sign meant only one thing. The chauffeur was challenging him to a race.

3

Mavor did a quick calculation. The Van Den Plas had the V12 Jaguar engine, bloody quick motor; the Jensen was a V8, but obviously would corner twice as fast as a huge limo. His heart suddenly beating faster. Yeah, he could do it. He looked at the chauffeur, raised his own right hand, closed the fingers, stuck up his thumb, and waited.

The lights changed to green.

Both drivers peaked their revs before they slammed home the clutches and burned rubber trails down the empty high street and out of the town.

The Cotswolds are hilly country, not high hills but an area criss-crossed by valleys. As if the Ice Age had ended there and piled up the junk that glaciers had pushed four hundred miles from Scotland. The rolling hills now the green-brown of early spring, sheep grazing on grass that had been hit by frost.

The Daimler was first away. It had fifty yards on Mavor in the first thousand yards out of the village. Eddie Mavor expected that. He kept the gear in third and the revs steady around the five thousand mark. He knew the road. He had a weekend cottage north of Gloucester. The Daimler was probably heading for some place like Wotton, or fashionable Thornbury. He would have at least around ten miles of road on which to crucify this optimist.

The Romans made Bath one of their principal cities and they settled as far west as Bristol. And they built their roads which were wide and straight. And there were wide and straight roads in Gloucestershire and Wiltshire. But the road that the Daimler and Mavor were racing on was something that had been a cart-track sometime in history and later just tarmacadamed over. It followed every contour of the land and twist of the valley.

Mavor slipstreamed the Daimler, marvelling first at the

speed of the huge car, then its road-holding, and then its driver, in that order. The chauffeur knew how to shift the bastard. They were both dealing with country lanes no more than fourteen feet wide, often narrower. That bloke with his V12 engine and his Harrod's standard light grey chauffeur's uniform with peaked cap must have picked up his driving on some race-track somewhere. But Mavor was no slouch— he'd done another type of racing. One of his proudest achievements was that, twice, the Richards' mob had used him as a wheelman on bank hold-ups, one involving a well-known dice with the Force.

An open stretch of road. The Daimler climbing now, using just four thousand revs to take it from ninety over the hundred an hour mark as it hit the peak of a hill.

'Jesus Christ,' Mavor said aloud, but barely audible above the howl of his own engine.

The Daimler sailed over the prow of the hill, and bottomed its suspension with a crunch on the slope beyond.

Mavor followed, mystified. It may have been an illusion, but as the Daimler went over the hill top a little of the weak sunlight did get through its front windscreen and the rear smoked glass, and Mavor thought for a second he saw two heads. Could there be two people in the Daimler, the peaked-hat chauffeur and someone in the back, in the smoked glass compartment?

It was time now to use the Jensen's superior road-holding, time to show the chauffeur and his pal, if there was another lunatic on the ride, that a limousine was no match for a piece of machinery that had been designed on the drawing-board as a sports car. Mavor knew that a half mile on and about five miles from Wotton the road went round a bend, widened, then went into a series of S-bends. That's where he'd take the Daimler.

5

His eyes sought the bend. His left hand on the gear shift, still in third, engine at five thousand. Then he slammed the gear into second, drifted the car through the bend, less than four feet separating him from the limousine. Then he de-clutched, peaked the revs at six and a half and punched the Jensen past the Daimler while the chauffeur was still lining it up and steadying it after the bend.

After that, it should've been a foregone conclusion. The Daimler never really had a chance. But the chauffeur wouldn't let up. Mavor in the Jensen, waltzing the car through S-bends, listening to the music of the engine, the screaming choir of tyres. It was the first time he'd really driven the car, and tested its guts against his. And they matched. And he was driving away from the huge black monster that was growing smaller in his driving mirror. But still there. And he was loving every second of it.

He hit the outskirts of Wotton. The traffic lights in the main square of the tiny town were red. He pumped the brakes and he brought the car cruising to a halt.

In his driving mirror he studied the Daimler entering the village fast, and coming up as if to line up behind him. But Mavor hoped the chauffeur would bring the big car along-side. Because as far as he was concerned the race was over. He'd clearly proven his and the Jensen's superiority.

The chauffeur brought the black limousine alongside. Mavor had ten seconds to study the man's impassive face, staring ahead, not looking at all in his direction. And then suddenly one of the smoked glass windows at the back of the limousine, the one nearest Mavor, powered down. And Mavor realized there *had* been a passenger in the back of the limo. . . .

The smoke-brown window slid right down and Mavor saw a face he didn't recognize. And he saw the 12-bore

6

sawn-off shotgun come up and turn on him about a second before it went off and blew most of his brains around the immaculate white pigskin interior of the Jensen.

Detective Inspector Jack Regan, Flying Squad, sat in Gennaro's Restaurant in Soho and watched his Scallopini Marsala go cold. He had ordered it. He couldn't eat it. He was thirty-six. He'd been eighteen years on the piss. But never ever a night like last night.

All he remembered was the full bottle of Jack Daniels which he'd seen off in the opening two hours of the Flying Squad Ball at Grosvenor House. He remembered that label, but not the others. And the hell of it was that he wasn't a drunkard. But just being around his colleagues socially made him nervous. And he'd worked out why last night. Before he went on to whatever it was after the Jack Daniels. What made him nervous around his colleagues was that they respected him, and he did not respect them. And that he had realized for the first time last night, and it was a hell of a lousy discovery.

And now tonight the Greek.

Theodoraki sat opposite him shoving spaghetti into his face as if a race was on. Theodoraki was eighteen stone of Greek crap, and a snout, which means a police informer, and a poor snout. But he knew some of the Thomson people, and Regan was on to that firm.

So he had called Theodoraki, where he worked in the bookie's in Romilly Street, and the bubble suggested Gennaro's. Like Gennaro's was expensive, and was going to take a lot of explaining as an incidental on the expenses side of his diary.

He pushed the Scallopini Marsala aside and studied the Greek, trying through the blazing hangover to work out an approach. But there was no way but the direct way. 'You know a bloke called Thomson. Frank Thomson. F.J. Thomson?'

'Yes,' the Greek said through the spaghetti, 'know the boy very good.'

'See him lately?'

'No lately.'

'How lately?'

Theodoraki shoved some Chianti in with the pasta, chewed the lot around and pretended to think. 'Four, five months ago, maybe.'

'Did he have money?' Regan asked casually.

'No money. You remember he had big chauffeur car? No car. And no cabs. I drop him at the bus depot, Victoria Station. No money.'

Regan took all that in and wondered about it. 'Then it'd surprise you if I told you he's been in Amsterdam and bought a hotel.'

'Amsterdam? Hotel?'

'Not a two-up two-down knocking shop, but a bloody great hotel on Dam Square.'

Theodoraki pretended for a moment he was bringing an intellect as powerful as Plato's on to the proposition. 'Impossible,' he announced, but his eyes were shifting like two trade winds, giving away that he knew all about such possibilities as hotels, and more besides.

'I want to know who financed Thomson to buy the hotel—I want to know why a hotel. I know it's probably a front for a blag. What blag? I think you can find out things. I'm going to give you a week. Then I'm going to come round to your flat in Dean Mews with those two nice young sergeants of mine who you know, and we're going to kick the shit out of you.'

Theodoraki choked on his spaghetti and grabbed for his glass of wine. 'But what have I done, Mr Regan?'

'Hand me your wallet,' Regan said firmly. Heads were beginning to turn in the restaurant; not that he was creating a scene, but obviously something was going on between the two men.

Theodoraki didn't argue. Regan opened Theodoraki's wallet. There were about fifty twenty-pound notes stuffed inside it. 'The taxpayer picks up the tab for this meal. Normally. This time you.'

He got up, dropped the Greek's wallet back on the table. He had seen Jules, the head waiter, on the opposite side of the room, answer a phone and turn and signal him. 'A week. Then you get a kicking. Or Thomson information. And for information about how you have a grand in your skite. Don't run away. That could become serious. . . .'

He left the Greek facing two ruined meals and crossed to Jules, and took the phone from him. It was his guvnor, Chief Inspector Haskins.

'Regan? Eddie Mavor's dead, near Wales. Shotgun. Friend of yours, yes?'

'No.'

'You knew him?'

'Snout of mine, occasionally. Perhaps four years back.'

'Why the shit? You knew him well. What is it? You don't want to get mixed up in a murder case?'

'He was a nobody, and he was a snout. There's nothing deader than a nobody snout that's ceased talking.'

'You're on the case. Till I take you off it.'

Regan concentrated on his hang-over. In some recess in the corner of his throbbing head there was a way out, an excuse to get off the case, but he couldn't think of it.

'Where are you?' Haskins asked.

9

'Gennaro's.'

'Have you got Len with you?'

'Yes. He's outside.'

'Do me a favour. Go to London Airport, pick up a man called Lieutenant Ewing, San Francisco Police, PA Flight 101, due 21.30. Take him to the Berkeley Hotel.'

Regan let a little pause creep into the conversation. He didn't like the style of delivery of the request, or its type. 'I'll see if I can fit that in. But just for the record, sir, I am not a fucking taxi service,' he said firmly.

Haskins was not intimidated. 'Welcome Lieutenant Ewing to our shores. He's looking for a gringo cop-killer in the Smoke. You're looking for a snout-killer in Wales or Gloucestershire. You've got lots of real words and common goals to discuss—'

Regan put the phone down on his boss. One day he was going to be fired for his insolence and insubordination. That would be when he lost his trump card. Detective Inspector Jack Regan's trump card was that he was the best detective in the Flying Squad, and possibly in the whole of London, and he had the record, the printed words, the statistics of cases solved, convictions made, to prove it.

He left Gennaro's without a backward glance at Theodoraki. His driver, Constable Len Roberts, sat in the Ford Consul. Regan climbed in beside him, carefully sat back, took out a bottle of Disprin, shoved in two, and chewed.

'Where to, guv?'

'London Airport.' Regan looked at his watch. 'No hurry. 21.30. Oceanic. We pick up a Yank lieutenant, San Francisco Police Department.'

'What's that about, guv?'

'Jesus alone knows.'

Len let the clutch in gently. In his eight years of driving

Regan he had learned how to exactly gauge the hang-overs —which were the ones where Regan was still speakable to; which the ones where you daren't say a word. Tonight was silent night.

James Purcell, alias Eddie Christopher, sat in his Curzon House Hotel suite, frustration building into real anger. He knew there was a plane out of London Heathrow to New York at midnight—got into Kennedy on or about two am. The way things were going, he would be on it.

He was annoyed because he had always had some lurking doubts about the enterprise. Then, when he got to London three days ago, the up-front money was there and that had temporarily reassured him. But no contact since. And he hated hotel rooms. And he couldn't leave it because these guys didn't call up and leave numbers to call back.

He had undergone a name and character transformation at London Airport. He'd had no trouble at Immigration or Customs and then had gone straight into the gents' lavatories, locked himself in a cubicle, unpacked his kit-bag with his battery shaver, and shaved off his moustache and sideburns. Then on to his nose a large pair of horn-rims. He compared the result in a pocket mirror that he also had with the shaving kit, with the photograph in a brand-new passport. He looked like Thompson.

The brand-new passport was in the name George Howard Thompson. That was the name he used when he registered at the Curzon House and picked up the big envelope containing the five thousand pounds sterling in cash.

He didn't stay in the suite all the forty-eight hours. He'd wandered the concourses, sat in the Coffee Shoppe. But always warning the switchboard that he could be paged—he would be in the hotel. He made one trip to the jeweller's by

11

the main doors and paid eight hundred pounds for a watch. Even for him, and he was used to easy money in quantities, two thousand dollars for a watch was bread. But it was a fine watch, or more accurately two watches. It was Kutchinsky—it had two dials under a single flat plate of clear amethyst, with just a hint of pink in it, which went well with the crackle-finish solid 22-carat gold case. A traveller's watch, so-called. One watch face showed the time in your country of origin, the other the country where you were. He noticed one watch dial read four o'clock. Four pm five days ago when he killed the lousy cop on the other side of the world.

It wasn't the first time he'd killed. By no means. But it was the first time he'd killed a cop. He still had a real hangover of nervousness about that.

He set one pair of hands on the Kutchinsky dial to London time, the other to New York time. That's where he'd be going if he cut out of this lousy town. He liked the watch. He missed his moustache. He'd taken four months to grow it. It suited him. He was tall and sparely built, attractive face but a little on the anonymous side of good looks. The moustache had set it off. The glasses and the hair he'd bleached before the plane flight put an extra eight years on him. He was thirty-eight. Now he looked forty-five.

It was six pm in the suite and he called room service for the twentieth time in his three days there. The service came fast—a BLT, root beer, coffee, and a side order of mixed salad, plus the same little waiter who was always so attentive.

He reckoned the waiter must think he was some kind of nut—always in the room, every three hours room service, more or less the same order every time.

12

'Good evening, Mr Thompson.' The little waiter pushed in a trolley that could have carried a feast for six. 'Your order, sir.'

'Thank you,' Purcell said. He was reading a copy of *Holiday Britain*, an incomprehensible magazine which was delivered free to the room and consisted of a hundred photographs of a technicolour country burning under a Saharan sun. This was supposed to be England? Purcell had been in London three times in his life. It had rained through all his visits. It was raining now.

'Shall I lay out your food for you, sir?' The waiter asked.

'No, leave it on the trolley. I'll roll the trolley out when I'm finished.'

'Shall I show you what I've got for you, sir?'

Purcell looked up from the magazine, puzzled. 'What d'you mean?'

'You'd like to see what we've brought you, sir?'

'You've brought me root beer, BLT, salad . . . that's what I ordered.'

'Extras, sir,' the little waiter said. He opened the door on the warm-box under the trolley. He pulled out a Smith and Wesson .38, a fifty-box of shells, and a continental-style, left-shoulder, leather-strapped canvas holster. He handed the three items to Purcell.

'Who the hell are you?' Purcell asked gently.

'One of your employers, sir,' the man replied. His voice had some regional accent Purcell didn't recognize. 'We had to check you out. We're sorry we kept you waiting two days—'

'Three,' Purcell corrected.

'Sorry, we are.'

'What happens now?'

'You will drink your coffee, sir, before it gets cold.'

'Fuck the coffee! What happens next?' Purcell's voice hard.

'You sit on your arse and you wait'—the voice of the waiter sharp, to match Purcell's—'and when we're ready we'll let you know. Maybe in an hour, maybe longer . . .'

'Who's we?'

The waiter shrugged away an answer.

'And what happens when you get round to calling me, friend?'

'I'll take you to the Broker.'

'And who or what's the Broker?' Purcell annoyed now, feeling he'd been caught on the hop by a London hotel waiter turning out to be the contact. It hadn't occurred to him as a possibility.

'Anything we feel you must know, we'll let you know. Do as you promised, stick the trolley out in the corridor when you're finished with it. We're always short of trolleys. Thoughtless bloody tourists, mostly Yanks, never putting 'em in the corridors . . . bastards . . .' the waiter said without any real feeling as he walked out. He closed the door firmly behind him.

Purcell took the gun, the shells and holster over to the cupboard and stored them in the smallest of his three suitcases. He went back, sat down and looked at the food. For some reason he couldn't understand, he suddenly didn't feel hungry.

Lieutenant John Ewing, San Francisco Police Department, turned out to be a tall man who gave very few words away. But Regan could work out a few things. He'd obviously been to England before. He wore a dark grey suit, white shirt, and club tie. There were frequent visitors at New Scotland Yard from the US, mostly FBI. They could be spotted at a distance of half a mile down Victoria Street—clothes too thin and lightweight for the English climate, always multicoloured socks. And the look of a race who went to their hairdressers daily, and had just a little too much trimmed off. Ewing's hair was long for a US cop. His clothes were New York Account Executive Madison Avenue. His age, Regan calculated, about forty. His voice was slow, quiet, and firm.

Regan showed his ident to one of the Special Branch men who took him through Customs and Immigration to pick Ewing up.

Regan made small talk. 'You have a good flight?'

The man didn't answer. Instead he paused for a moment whilst the Immigration people punched his passport with a rubber stamp, and then, turning his slow blue eyes on Regan, like he was noticing him for the first time: 'Anything new on Purcell?'

'Nothing more than the telex at 09.00 this morning.'

Ewing nodded. He'd received the telex.

'He came to London Airport. He landed as James Purcell. Immigration Officer asked him purpose of visit. He

15

remembers the man said "business talks". Immigration stamped him two months. You want to talk to the officer?'

Ewing shook his head, picked up his briefcase, and headed for Customs.

Regan could see the bulge under Ewing's left shoulder. Nonetheless he couched it as a question. 'Mr Ewing, are you armed?'

Ewing looked at him and nodded.

'Small formality. The serial number of your gun.' Regan was already signalling a young Customs Officer and pointing towards a cubicle. He steered Ewing towards the cubicle. 'Things get stolen in hotels. Including guns. Regulations. All serial numbers of all guns entering the country.'

The US detective shrugged. From his expression it was obvious he considered his time was being wasted. There was another unspoken question in the expression. Did he look to Regan like somebody who'd leave his gun lying around a hotel to get stolen?

They walked into the opaque glass cubicle. Regan asked for the gun. Ewing pulled it out and handed it across. It was a Navy Colt .45.

'Lieutenant Ewing of the San Francisco Police will be with us for some time.'

'Yes, sir.' The Customs Officer was young and enthusiastic. He took the gun to the desk lamp and read off the serial number on the stock and made a note of it on a piece of paper. Ewing still a blank face of controlled impatience.

'Sorry about this. I think you've been to England before. You appreciate we invented red tape.' Regan tried to make light of it.

'Any ammunition for this revolver, sir?' the young Customs Officer asked.

16

Ewing reached in his right-hand jacket pocket and pulled out a clear plastic tear-off pack—official PD issue—containing a dozen shells.

The Customs man took them and examined them. Regan saw his sudden reaction. Regan reached across and took the plastic pack from the Customs man. Each of the .45 shells must have been placed in a vice and an X cut with a hacksaw across the business end of the bullet. When fired, the shell would spread and blow a hole three inches wide through any part of a man, instead of a half-inch hole.

'Dumdum bullets,' Regan said. 'I know they're not legal in war.' He turned and looked at the Customs Officer. The young bloke shrugged.

Regan handed the plastic roll back to the visitor. 'Can I ask you why you cut bullets into dumdums?'

The American took his time, then decided his answer. 'If I shoot someone in San Francisco, Mr Regan, I shoot to kill 'em.' He said it quietly. 'Otherwise I don't shoot at all.'

It was the first time he had been genuinely communicative since his arrival in England.

They picked up Purcell at ten o'clock. Two men, one the little room service waiter, the other a man of average height but very broad, with a bald head on a bull neck. Purcell and the waiter's friend were not introduced. The waiter's friend may have been important; on the other hand he may just have been the chauffeur. He drove the battered Austin Cambridge from the hotel west to Fulham. Their destination a pub in the Fulham Road.

The place was crowded. It had been a long time since Purcell had been in a crowded English pub. The smell hit him again—a smell like a marine company sergeants' mess after manoeuvres, sweat and beer and men. The little hotel waiter began chattering on in a nondescript way, remarks about weather, horses, tomorrow's winners, and an attempt to explain to Purcell, who knew all about it and wasn't interested anyway, the business of English Pools and how people made fortunes winning them.

They were clearly waiting for somebody, the little waiter and the driver. The somebody didn't turn up.

Closing time. The drunks in the nightly ritual with the barmaids about that one last drink, and snarling at the historic refusal. Slurred voices in a loud blanket of good-byes and good-will among those not blind drunk. Everybody beginning to filter noisily out. Now it was clear that the somebody who was supposed to turn up hadn't, Purcell began to get annoyed. The little waiter, ignoring the American's stony look, went off to make a phone call. He came back. 'You're cleared,' he said.

'What the hell is that supposed to mean?'

'The man came here half an hour ago and looked you over. You're who you say you are. We'll go now to his house.'

'What man? What house? And you said you'd checked me out already?'

The little man answered one of the questions. 'So you've been checked again. People get killed in this game. I've got a vested interest in staying alive. Five more years I get me Curzon House pension coming. Come on.'

Then they were driving through night London, this time heading north. Purcell would have liked to know the areas they were passing through, but he didn't ask. He knew the centre of London quite well. After a big job in America he'd often gone Londonwards or elsewhere in Europe for the cooling off period—in fact he felt he'd invented the device. A bank is heisted in some backwoods in Wisconsin—the

18

cops don't turn their attention immediately to looking for the thief in Bruxelles or London. First they look locally, then they look interstate. Purcell considered it his trademark. He was sure the FBI, who were mostly interested in his activities, bank robberies being Federal offences, did not know this trademark.

He saw a liquor store. It had a sign on it—BRENT WINE AND SPIRITS. He tried to remember what he'd read about Brent. He decided it amounted to nothing.

The house was in a street off Brent High Street. It looked unoccupied. Two of the lower front windows were broken. The garden gate was hanging on to one hinge.

The door was opened by a man who'd have to bow his head to get through most doors. He was several inches over six feet and white haired. He'd be about fifty. His face was expressionless. 'Welcome to London, Mr Purcell. My name is James.' He extended a hand to Purcell's arm and led him down the dim lit corridor to a room at the rear of the ground floor. There were other doors off the hall, all open, showing dirty bare rooms without carpets or furniture.

It was a surprise then for the American when he followed the man into the last room. It was comfortably, almost luxuriously furnished. A single furnished room in an empty house—Purcell wondered about that. The man indicated that Purcell should sit in a deep leather armchair, then pointed to a drinks cabinet. Purcell shook his head.

'We'll get straight to the point,' the man said. 'We should give you some facts on the political aspects of the venture we're about to embark on.'

'I'm not interested in your politics,' Purcell said quietly.

The big man studied him, no expression, but nodding slowly. 'We don't give a tit whether you are or not. The distinction that I must state and you must understand, is

19

we're not just another bunch of bank robbers. We're politically motivated.'

'And I'm not interested in politics,' Purcell said again, softly and firmly.

'Don't you see I'm trying to tell you something that might affect the way you draft this job, something that could fundamentally affect your approach?'

'What are you saying?'

'These fifteen men you get to pull this job, they're not just robbers, they're soldiers. Disciplined soldiers. They will take risks that professional robbers wouldn't take.'

Purcell nodded slowly. 'Okay, I get that. Now a key question which was never answered by your contact man in New York. I want an answer now.' He studied the tall man. 'Why me?'

'Because you're the best draftsman in the world, our professional informants tell us.'

'The real reason,' Purcell insisted.

'You know what we plan to hit in London. Not an English bank, but an American one. We have a lot of grass roots sympathy in America.'

'What d'you mean "grass roots sympathy"?'

'If something goes wrong we don't want it to look like one of our operations, but a professional job planned, drafted by a professional American, working in London. D'you understand?'

'What's going to go wrong?' Purcell asked softly.

'The Honourable Mrs Astor booked a cruise to New York. Nothing could go wrong; in fact the ship *Titanic* was designed in such a way that it couldn't sink. If the raid that you research and set up goes wrong, you're an American bank-raider who organized certain people to rob banks in London.'

Purcell took the point. 'When do I start?'

'We're ready to go. You tell us.'

The interview was over. The tall man decided that for the two of them, and got up.

'What happened to the other draftsman you used, the one who took more than his share?'

The tall man turned his hard eyes on the American. 'Inquest's at Gloucester tomorrow, Mr Purcell.'

Detective Inspector Jack Regan sat through the inquest and wondered what the hell he should tell the local nick. A murder squad had been set up at Gloucester under a Superintendent Rosswell. Rosswell was a small fat man who stuck his right hand in the centre flap of his jacket like Napoleon Bonaparte. But if Napoleon had had a mind as slow as Rosswell's he would have just made lieutenant by Elba. Regan had spent two hours with him, from nine to eleven am. It had been like a year.

What could you say to Rosswell and his squad about Eddie Mavor? No real point in saying more than the coroner's jury would conclude: 'Murder by a person or persons unknown.' Mavor had done it all. Name the crime, Mavor had a finger, arm or boot in it at some point over his thirty-seven years: grievous bodily harm, housebreaking, big-steal robbery, blackmail, perjury, vice of every shade, shape, size and description, including reverse white-slavery—whores from Beirut, Turkey, and Greece, to London. And blue movies, in some of which parts of him had appeared, and not the parts you saw in a Doris Day film.

Then there were the hard times, when Mavor couldn't get it together. And there were five pubs in the Bermondsey area where he could be bought drinks by his friendly neighbourhood policemen in plain clothes. And sometimes more than a drink—sometimes a tenner slipped under the table when the poor bastard, on his fifth vodka straight before lunch, would stop talking about himself and his mates in the glorious past, and would start talking about his mates and their acquaintances in the future. 'D'you know that Aussie villain, 'Arry Avon, down the Mile End, selling more bastard radios than Sony have, in this Queen's country this annum. And no bastard wonder, 'cos he's nicked the lot. Seven thousand Sony Sports Elevens; a fiver, a kick up the arse, and he'll even service the sodding things. . . .'

Sometime in January 1967 Regan met him. Regan a Detective Sergeant then, in the Flying Squad. Some bloody madman had thieved a pantechnicon containing eleven thousand dozen packets of Tampax. The *News of the World* got hold of it—made it into a funny ha-ha joke item. Regan was in the doghouse with his bosses at the time. He'd stepped on some DI's corns at the Yard. So he got slung 'The Case of the Missing Tampons.' It pissed him off for two months.

He got some clues that moved him south of the river. Then the Bermondsey nick suggested Mavor as a possible information source. Mavor had done it for five tenners and a bottle of Smirnoff. The connection he made with Mavor at a personal level was sound. The man liked and trusted him. Within weeks, Mavor's calls to the yard and pub chats were producing real results and that's what it's all about. Because most of the promises of information from such sources are like dressed crab, all dress, no meat.

From '67 to '69 Mavor and his fortunes lived in the valley. Then at the end of '69 he took off for a peak. And he made it. And his calls to the Yard stopped. And then it was other snouts talking about Mavor. 'Saw him in a Roller the other night—brand-new vehicle. White. Didn't match his girl—coon. That TV singer, personality, what's 'er name. . . ?' And Mavor was into the high life, and running some clubs, and property companies, and paying a certain amout of Income Tax. Fraud Squad looked him over in 1970, and decided whatever rackets he was into weren't too bent. They'd bear him in mind, rather than foot around testing for pressure-points.

Jack Regan got a call in February 1971 from Mavor saying some mick, who was giving him agro, was the collector on some regular dock-thieving game out of King George V docks. It was a good tip. Regan got the mick, and six lock-up garages containing twenty grand of Heinz's 57 Varieties, i.e., every kind of stolen goods from copper pipe to digital electric clocks. But it was the last time he heard about Eddie Mavor until the day Mavor paid somebody a debt in a Jensen in Wotton.

So what do you say to Superintendent Rosswell? A man who lived on his wits, lost them, spread about the interior of a luxury car. On the man's CRO file, a report indicating that he'd done small services for the Force, and naming Regan as contact. Rosswell had a murder squad but he didn't really know where to start on a London villain. He didn't want the Yard crashing in, but he didn't mind Regan because he'd sussed the man's lack of interest.

Regan was not interested for two reasons. A villain gets killed by another villain. That villain's going to get chopped by the CID sooner or later for other villainies. Also Mavor had stopped giving him information long ago, so he felt no real connection, like he'd been chatting with Mavor two days ago and then the bastard is topped.

Regan listened to the coroner's summing up—another very boring man. He checked his watch—two pm. There would be time to view the mortal remains at Gloucester Mortuary, and be back in London around six or seven.

There was only one minute stirring of slightest interest in Regan's mind about Mavor's exit. Shotgun at close range in the main square of a bloody village, broad daylight, no one in sight, no witnesses. That sounded like a cool kill. It sounded like professionals. And Regan was always interested in professionals. He was one himself.

Detective Chief Inspector Haskins didn't know what to make of Lieutenant Ewing of the San Francisco Police. First of all he thought it might be a problem of rank. There is the fact that a simple lieutenant in the American CID can be a very elevated individual, depending on his personal reputation and where he works from. Haskins had met lieutenants in New York who wielded more power than their captains, DA's, or Congressmen. At first he thought that was why Ewing was cold towards him—perhaps Ewing thought that his contact at the Flying Squad should be at superintendent-level.

There was another factor. Haskins knew from long experience of contact with Yank cops at Scotland Yard that they regarded their trips to London as a gravy train. They might be looking for some real bastard US killer. However, once in London, they never forgot to enjoy themselves. US cops were turning up in Flying Squad offices, New Scotland Yard, perhaps half a dozen a year. And more, recently, as everybody now accepted that Interpol was falling apart at the seams. So these blokes came to London and they enjoyed themselves. So why, Haskins wondered, was Ewing such a pain in the arse?

On the morning after his arrival Ewing requested a working breakfast with Haskins. Ewing suggested his hotel; Haskins accepted. The eating part of the breakfast was made agonizing by Ewing's simple device of refusing to say a word. Haskins found himself in the unreal position of the chatterbox sounding off about ways and means for the visitor to locate his quarry in England. The nearest Ewing got to even acknowledging Haskins' presence was a slight nod from time to time. He said more to the waiter about how the bacon should be real crispy, like almost burned, than he said to the senior English policeman.

They were well into their second coffee when Ewing at last spoke. 'I knew Denny,' he said.

Haskins' eyes queried the introduction of a so far unmentioned name.

'Dennis O'Hagen. The guy Purcell executed.'

Haskins now thought he had the clue to the man's mood and silence. 'A close friend?'

Ewing, eyes thoughtful, as if really considering the depth of the relationship for the first time. 'Not so close. A buddy.'

'It's never happened to me in the Force,' Haskins said gently. 'The murder of a colleague that I knew as a friend. Can I ask you, how does it hit?'

'I can speak only for me.' It was the first time Ewing was really conversing. 'I don't care about a dead man, because it's illogical—they're beyond care. What I care about is their wives and children. O'Hagen had no children. He'd just gone through a lousy divorce—stunk.' He paused for a moment. 'So you ask me what do I feel about Denny O'Hagen? I feel I got a job on. Find Purcell, get him Stateside. Get him in a court. Other than that I don't feel anything.'

To Square One, Haskins thought. Ewing's just a cold fish. He hadn't met a lot of them but undoubtedly they must exist. Ewing was obviously a clever man, but he had no feelings, and that was in a way demonstrated by his conversational reticence. You had to feel enthusiasm to talk about anything. Haskins felt all this but at the same time made a mental note not to dismiss this man's character with such bald explanations. There were always other elements. Haskins decided to reserve judgment on Ewing until he knew him better. And he would know him better because his boss, Superintendent Maynon, had said: 'I want you to really look after this chap. I spent two very happy months care of the Frisco PD in 1965, with a man called Ed Renly, who's now Chief there. When Ewing goes back he'll tell Ed you didn't fail in your helpfulness and your hospitality.'

The next thing the reticent Ewing said hit Haskins between the eyes like a blow from a fist.

'O'Hagen was a long-time policeman, old timer, knew a lot of guys. They've thrown some dollars together. They've put up fifty thousand—that's roughly twenty thousand pounds on the rate of exchange. I'd like you to spread the news around. . . .'

'What do you mean, spread the news around?' Haskins asked carefully.

'The first of you British cops to get a bead on Purcell gets ten thousand pounds. The other ten thousand pounds is on offer to your informers and your underworld for information.'

Haskins couldn't avoid the schoolteacher voice. 'No English policeman is allowed to take that kind of money for doing his job.'

'You didn't have to say that, Chief Inspector,' Ewing said. He had turned away and called out to a waiter for a third coffee, then turned back to Haskins. 'Between ten and twenty thousand is available for the information that grabs Purcell. Now if you're going to quote me regulations it's because you're a senior officer and you have to be an official person.'

'I'm not quoting you regulations in the abstract: no English policeman is allowed to touch your money.'

'Put it this way. I don't know how long it'll take, but when

I leave England I expect to have Purcell. And I don't expect to have the money.'

Detective Chief Inspector Haskins was anxious to get the meal over and get back to the Yard. He was anxious to report to his boss, Superintendent Maynon, that he thought Lieutenant Ewing was a dangerous man.

It so happened that they had a use for a dangerous man in the Flying Squad, to deal with an entirely separate matter.

Jack Regan stood in Gloucester City Mortuary and studied the corpse of Eddie Mavor. The body had been washed a couple of times in forty-eight hours and the head turned right-profile by some bland mortician. The head was turned right-profile because the left profile was still in the Jensen. It would be a bland, experienced mortician who had turned that head, probably because he'd been present over the years on too many occasions when people, including policeman, had vomited whilst viewing mutilated remains.

The mortician wasn't there. The Exhibits Officer was. Regan went from the cold slab over to the table where Mavor's clothing and effects were laid out.

'Your name?'

'Detective Sergeant Randwell, sir.' The DS was about twenty-five years old and gave off enough nervousness to suggest this was his first day at work, and if he didn't get his answers right, it might be his last.

Regan studied the table with the personal effects and the swab test-tubes. Trousers, jacket, pants, each item of clothing in a separate paper bag. A wallet, keys, driving licence, some papers, these in separate little polythene bags. 'Shoes?'

The Exhibits Officer selected one of the paper bags and brought out an expensive pair of Italian-made shoes. Regan turned them over. He was looking for mud on the soles. He wanted to know if Mavor had stopped off anywhere on the M4 motorway from the time he left his night-club in London —this time had now been established by one of his employees—up to his death in Wotton. Any stops he made off the M4 would more likely have been to villages or farms. There was not a trace of countryside mud or grass on the shoes. It was a matter of no significance. It was just Regan's logical approach to any corpse—begin at its extremities.

'Now swabs.' He looked at the stoppered test-tubes in a wooden rack. 'What swabs did you get?'

'Usual, sir—nose-swabs and swabs from under each fingernail, sir.'

Regan looked along the line of test-tubes. Each test-tube labelled: 'index finger left,' 'index finger right,' and so on. 'Anything obvious from the fingernail swabs?'

'No, sir,' the young sergeant said, his voice slowly gaining confidence. 'Except he took a little while to die. On the basis that there is little to get a swab from under three of the nails, because he broke them in death throes.'

'Why d'you say that?' Regan hated inexperienced coppers making sweeping statements.

'Well, it seemed an obvious explanation to me, sir.'

'He could've broken his nails grappling with his killer,' Regan suggested.

'I suppose so, sir.'

'Where are the swabs from the area around the head-wound?' Regan asked.

The young sergeant went pale. 'What swabs, sir?'

Regan groaned inwardly. 'Are you telling me the body's been washed and there are no swabs from the head-wound area?'

'I wasn't asked, sir.' The young officer's face now going from pale to pink.

'So now we'll never know whether he was shot close up, with powder particles round the wound, struggling with his murderer and breaking his nails in the process, and maybe

31

the struggle being seen or heard by witnesses—or whether he was dropped in a second by a first-class marksman.'

The sergeant was now visibly trembling. 'The Chief Superintendent didn't ask me to take swabs of the wound, sir.'

'Nobody had to ask you, Sergeant,' Regan snapped. 'The Chief Super doesn't come into it. You're the Exhibits Officer. You've missed an extremely important swab. Why don't you just go away—get out of here.'

The young sergeant didn't attempt a monosyllable of defence. He went.

Regan located the brown paper bag containing the jacket of Mavor's suit. It was bespoke, but the tag came from a well-known West End company. There were some East End tailors who made suits for robbers, with extras like secret pockets in the fold of the armpit or in the shoulder padding. Regan went through all the pockets again. The Gloucester police had missed nothing—cleaned out. Regan moved to the polythene bags that contained the contents of Mavor's pockets. The first contained a wallet. It was an expensive Dunhill wallet, crocodile leather, gold-cornered. It contained three brand-new twenty-pound notes, driving licence, endorsed twice for speeding, car insurance, and a slim, leather-backed note-pad which Mavor had used as his telephone book. Perhaps a hundred names, companies, telephone numbers in it—mostly around London—enough to keep Rosswell's murder squad busy for at least a month. Each address written in Mavor's spidery, illiterate hand. He'd written one address in the Shell Building on the Embankment as Room 505, spelling it 'Shel' Building. He'd spelt Marylebone High Street 'Marlbone High St'. Then, stuck in the middle of his address book, a page torn from a book of matches. On one side, the book of matches advertised a night-club, the Glory Hole. On the other side an address: 14 Carlyle Buildings, Jamaica Road, SE 1.

Regan picked up the typed notes that one of Rosswell's staff or maybe the Exhibits Officer had made. He had listed the exhibits of the various swabs, noted that nothing of obvious interest had been found, but they would be sent on to the forensic experts for analysis. Then he had copied out, this time a little more literately, the contents of the address pad, and numbered the hundred and thirty addresses it contained. The address on the back of the book of matches was listed last.

Regan studied the police notes, then studied the back of the book of matches. The first thing that intrigued him about it was that he'd heard about the Glory Hole night-club. It had opened three weeks ago. He had yet to go there, but he could make one assumption. That Mavor went there, met somebody, wrote an address on the book-matches with the idea presumably of transferring it later to the address pad. This address was possibly the last Mavor ever collected.

The second thing that intrigued him was the way the Exhibits Officer or the Gloucester Police clerk had interpreted the address. It was the way Mavor wrote his fours—the style where the upright is a diagonal which joins at the top of the second upright. But Mavor's handwriting was spidery and imprecise. Regan was sure the number was four. The Gloucester lot had written it as nine, which it did look a lot like.

So they were going to look up 19 Carlyle Buildings, Jamaica Road SE 1, when the address Mavor had written was 14.

Regan didn't want to spend another two year-like hours with Superintendent Rosswell explaining the 'four' for 'nine' theory. He would get his Sergeant Carter to phone Gloucester CID. He did a quick check through the other polythene and paper bags. Nothing he could see of obvious interest—definitely forensic laboratory stuff now.

There was one other thing that intrigued him about the address Mavor had written on the book of matches. All the other addresses in the address pad reflected Mavor's recent life of ease and plenty, addresses of his fellow night-club owners, and new, powerful friends and showbiz people—no addresses at all from his old life of the Bermondsey days of poverty relieved by fivers and tenners slipped by Regan under a pub table. Except for that address. Regan knew Carlyle Buildings off the Jamaica Road—a crime ghetto in the last of real slum London. The last address Mavor collected was one from his past. Regan didn't want anything to do with this dead snout. He wanted to get on with Theodoraki the Greek, and the man who had just bought a hotel in Dam Square, Amsterdam. Nonetheless, there was something there that was just interesting enough. Regan knew he'd look up the address that the Gloucester Police had got wrong. He didn't know why, but he knew he'd do it.

But he didn't look up the address 14 Carlyle Buildings. Torrential rain hit the M4 all the way back to London. In France or Italy at the first sign of a cloud burst the motorist automatically accelerates to ninety miles an hour. The English, a population raised in howling and brawling gales, have never got used to driving in them, and reduce speed to a bumper to bumper twenty mile an hour crawl. Regan was supposed to get back to the Yard by five. He got to London at seven.

He stopped off at a phone kiosk in Hammersmith to make two calls. The first to Tanya. She'd been away for two weeks at some Trade Fair in Germany. She had told him, when she

34

left, specifically when she'd be back—he'd forgotten except that it was one day this week. He phoned and she was in, and sounded as if she'd be pleased to see him. The relationship had been having its problems recently. 'But don't tell your office at the Yard that you're at my number. D'you understand, Jack?'

Regan understood. He phoned Squad Office at the Yard and left Tanya's number with the switchboard. The switchboard operator said that Regan's immediate guvnor, DCI Haskins, urgently wanted to speak to him. Regan instructed the operator that Tanya's telephone number was for the convenience of everyone except Haskins.

He drove on from Hammersmith, east, and then north up Exhibition Road, through Hyde Park to Bayswater Road.

She lived in a small block of flats about a quarter of a mile from Marble Arch, buried in the hinterland of modern high-rises and quiet Victorian squares. Regan punched the entry phone. The door buzzed and he took the lift to the third floor. There were only four floors.

She greeted him a little coolly. He saw why. The cockney cleaning lady who 'did' for her was just finishing up her stint, and washing out the dusters. There was little else they could do for ten minutes while the important duster washing and terminal tidying away was completed.

Regan's eyes weighed her up. Her eyes were alert and hungry, her face paler than usual. She had no make-up. That meant she'd decided she'd want him immediately and had already wiped off the war-paint.

He'd left Gloucester four hours ago.

Slow car journeys fatigued him; the traffic had been appalling. He wasn't feeling particularly like sex, but was prepared to put on a show.

He felt her fine eyes critically on him. Over the last twelve months she'd been grooming him by suggesting the clothes she'd like him to wear. Dark suits, with a good, large-patterned silk tie, '*comme* Prince Windsor', she would say; Italian shoes. She'd bought him a present of a dozen pairs of silk socks from Cardin in Paris. He knew tonight he passed the test. He wore a dark blue suit, dark blue socks, black shoes, and a big blue tie with red polka dots on it. She'd bought the tie as well.

Mrs Mop took five minutes over her good-byes and what cleaning materials were running short, then the front door closed.

They kissed briefly. He broke it off. They moved across the hall into the bedroom.

In the bedroom he stripped her immediately and wordlessly, and led her to the large bed.

She, as always on these occasions when they'd been separated for two weeks—and that was a long time for them—was keyed up almost to desperation, and this made Regan suddenly hot and uncomfortable even though they made love naked and uncovered. And then immediately afterwards he was cold and shivering as the night air from the open window caught him. Manoeuvring off her and getting out of bed was a collection of awkward motions full of their elbows digging each other and a jar to his knee from some wooden edge. He had a shower and hoped she wouldn't join him. She didn't. He came back into the room wanting to find that perhaps she'd dozed off. She sometimes did after their sex. She was wide awake, and taking the pillow out from underneath her.

'You miss me?'

Regan nodded.

'Really?' she said with a toss of her shoulders. 'Then why do you make love to me as if you were in the other room?'

He met her eyes, and put on an expression as if to dismiss the question as nonsense. He stood his ground, drying himself, while she worked out something in silence.

'Are you tired of me?' She said it in a practical way.

'No.'

'I think two years is a long time for a love affair. I think you are tiring of me. . . .'

'Not true at all.' He spoke the words gently.

She considered this, first pursing her lips and then putting her head to one side, watching him. 'You didn't even notice.'

'What?'

She decided not to answer him, climbed out of bed and went into the shower.

Ten minutes later she was back, drying herself, duplicating the water pools that he'd sown across the carpet. She now looked much younger than her twenty-eight years. 'I put aloes in my womb.'

'What's that?' Regan was pouring himself a drink from a tray on a coffee table.

'It's a preparation. I bought it in a sex shop in Stuttgart. It makes the passage smaller. They said it gives it more satisfaction. Yes?'

He felt on the point of annoyance. She was in one of her challenging moods. He didn't feel like being forced into responses. He felt tired. He said quietly: 'I always enjoy our times together and I'm touched by the trouble you take.'

He took his drink over to the bedside table, then lay down with her. For a few minutes she said nothing, but suddenly her mood changed; she was looking content, her eyes unfocused on the ceiling.

'My beautiful after-sex cigarette.' She inhaled on it deeply. 'You know I have sometimes thought about this cigarette while we've been making love. The thought of it right in my mind.'

37

The phone by the bed rang. Her face turned to fury. She reached out, grabbed the phone and threw it down on the pillow beside him.

She slammed out of bed, grabbed up a dressing-gown, went through the door and banged that closed with enough force to shake the walls.

It was Carter on the phone. 'How did it go in Gloucester, guv?'

'Carlyle Buildings, Jamaica Road.' Regan lay back in bed, picked up Tanya's cigarette from the ashtray where it smouldered, and inhaled. 'Know it?'

'Den of thieves. Ted Miller, Harry Johnson—among others—in residence, when not at her Majesty's addresses.'

'I want something done fast and efficient.' Regan looked up at the ceiling thoughtfully, as if suddenly he had a doubt that Carter could do something speedily, efficiently. Carter was twenty-eight, not Bramshill, that élite embryo officer training outfit, but Dollis Hill, a suburb of London where Regan had poached him from the local CID. He'd poached Carter because he'd heard, and then checked, that Carter was efficient, hard, opinionated, right, honest, clever, and could work on his own. It was really only the last of these talents that Regan needed. Regan was a rare policeman in the Flying Squad—his superiors would describe him as a complete anomaly. The Flying Squad was an élite group of two hundred selected detectives, the backbone of Scotland Yard, who had a single identity that came from working closely together. But Regan, the DI with the best record of arrest and conviction, was a one-man show. DCI Haskins and Superintendent Maynon hated him for it. He had bucked the system and had made it work. They hated him also because the people Regan picked to work for him,

38

brought in from outside Squad Office, were minor Regans. And they were transferred to Squad on Regan's insistence, and they went wrong at some point because Regan wouldn't chaperone them, and then finally he'd get rid of them in some endless quest to find one Detective Sergeant who'd function exactly the way he wanted him to.

Carter not only fulfilled all Regan's needs, he fulfilled them too well. Carter would bear watching. Carter was after his job and the position that he, Regan, had pioneered—Regan the loner, the joker in the pack, too efficient to hold back, too ordered to take other people's orders. But on results, one of the top five DIs in London. They can't touch you if you're the best. That was Carter's goal, to be better, and even more isolated than Regan. At least that's what Regan decided. '14 Carlyle Buildings, relates to Eddie Mavor. You read the files while I was in Gloucester?'

'Yes, guv.'

'If Number 14 is occupied, search. If it's unoccupied, take it to pieces. I'm wiped out or I'd come with you.'

'All right, I'll try and find the duty JP.'

Regan looked at his watch. It was nine-fifteen. 'If the place is occupied, talk your way in; if unoccupied, use your God-given brute force. A door is a door. . . .'

Carter was probably opening his mouth for a smart answer when Regan put the phone down.

He got dressed and walked into the sitting-room. She was pouring herself a vodka straight. 'I'm on a very important case,' he said.

'I don't care any more about your very important cases.' She went to the window, looked down over the square, knocked back the vodka in half a dozen gulps, ignoring him.

'Is this whole bloody evening ruined?' he asked.

'Yes,' she said flatly, 'if the phone rings again for you, and it will ring—yes, the whole bloody evening is ruined.'

'You know the score.' He said it softly. 'The job I work on, I have to be available on the end of a phone twenty-four hours a day.'

'If you can't screw your girl and lie in her arms without the bloody phone ringing, you will end up totally inhuman.'

'I don't want to start that discussion now.'

'Well I do!' she said, anger mounting in her voice.

He picked up his raincoat and walked out of the flat.

Lieutenant Ewing had come away from his working breakfast with Detective Chief Inspector Haskins with the distinct impression that he had failed to make his point.

His three colleagues back home in SFPD who had started the fund had performed no mean feat. Fifty thousand dollars had been raised within the Department inside a week. That worked out at nearly ten dollars from every cop, clerk and coolie in the outfit.

Lieutenant Ewing knew the rules in England—Haskins didn't have to point them out.

The idea had been to acquaint Haskins with the news, so he could quietly whisper it around, that highly unofficial money was available for results. If a cop got a slight clue which would involve a lot of following up, he might do it if there was the prod of some dollars. Haskins had informed him in so many words that human nature wasn't the same the world over. Ewing did not believe Haskins. But there it was.

Not that anybody in the SFPD set himself up as an expert on the 'chaps' at New Scotland Yard; but rumours had reached Northern California in recent years that detectives in London no longer wore stiff white collars and bowler hats.

Word was that the Yard had changed, enlarged its horizons, got it together, and pulled itself fast into the middle of the twentieth century.

He had been in London eight years before, for a month. It had been the honeymoon of his second lousy marriage. Six weeks after London, where they screwed a lot, he had the doctors check, and the suspicions of his first wife were confirmed. He was sterile—by no means impotent—just one hundred per cent sterile. His second wife left him after a year.

For that London visit, his Chief at SFPD had fixed him up with an intro note to some guy at Scotland Yard. The guy had given him a quick look over the old Scotland Yard building on the river and smiled a lot; it was an hour's hospitality and that was that. Ewing had not been able to form any impression of the workings of the British police.

But, back home, a lot of guys who knew said that lately there had been changes. So Haskins had been a disappointment.

After the breakfast, he had left the hotel, found a cabby, asked him did he know any left-wing bookstores, and did he understand what was meant by left-wing bookstores? The cabby said he did and off they went.

An hour and a half later he was back at the hotel with half a dozen cheaply printed magazines.

He had then looked up Yellow Pages (Central) under 'security organizations'. He had dialled the first of twenty listed companies. 'Are you the largest security company in London?' Ewing had asked. The reply had come back honest and negative. 'Then who is?'

The reply came back that SECURCOM was the largest security business in London and England. Lieutenant Ewing

41

had phoned SECURCOM and had explained his position and asked for an appointment with a senior executive urgently.

They had suggested he meet Mr Elmount at eight pm that night.

At eight pm exactly, Lieutenant Ewing walked into Elmount's office in the SECURCOM headquarters in the Strand. It took Ewing about ten minutes to explain who he was, and about Purcell, and the killing, and the reward.

Mr Elmount was a large man who smoked thin cigars. At the end of Ewing's explanation he offered one to the Lieutenant. Ewing declined. 'So what exactly can we of SECURCOM do for you Lieutenant?'

'I want to find a man. I'm working with Scotland Yard. They're slow. I have limited time.' He paused to make quite sure that Elmount was following him. 'There are in London certain crime ghettos, right? Brixton, the East End, Fulham . . .'

Elmount was nodding.

'I want to discuss with you how much it would cost say to take thirty of your operatives and send them tonight into these ghettos to spread the word that I, Lieutenant Ewing of San Francisco, am in London and staying at the Bayswater Hotel, and would like to meet a Mr James Purcell.'

Elmount sucked on the cigar. 'It would cost a good deal of money to have thirty men doing that. May I ask you why you want that particular information dispersed?'

The big American nodded slowly as if he thought it was a reasonable question. 'It's clay-pigeon shooting. I set myself up as a clay-pigeon. If there's a shot, at least I'll know he's there. And I hope to see what direction the shot comes from.'

This is what Detective Sergeant Carter did in seven hours, from nine-fifteen pm to four-fifteen am—and a good example of the kind of efficiency that Regan approved of, and worried about.

At nine-thirty pm, having determined that there was no one answering the front door of the flat, 14 Carlyle Buildings, he'd gone up the fire escape at the rear of the building, lifted his right foot to the height of the lock and kicked at the door, tearing the Yale lock out of its gate.

A little old woman had catapulted out of the kitchen door of the adjoining flat and started screaming. 'Robbers, thief. Stop thief!'

Carter had studied Sarah Bernhardt reincarnated and marvelled at the noise of it all. He'd then produced his police ident. This had calmed her. She went off, she said, to make a cup of tea—would he like one? He'd said no.

The flat was three rooms, two of which were bedrooms and empty—not even bed linen on the bed. A kitchen, deserted and damp, and a living-room. Someone had recently moved out in a hurry. So fast in fact that he'd left a bottle of Glenlivet Highland Malt Whisky, which Carter had done some quality sampling on while he studied the other features of the interior *décor*—including a cold cup of coffee and a green mould sandwich. This, together with a half-packed suitcase, promoted the idea of the possible high speed departure of the last tenant.

Carter had wrapped a kitchen drying-cloth round his right hand, not to damage fingerprints, and had very carefully taken out, piece by piece, and spread on the bed, the contents of the suitcase. A man's suit, good cloth, good tailor. Some other clothes, socks, pants, shaving-gear, and four passports.

It was difficult opening the passports and trying not to smudge possible prints. They were Irish passports, looked genuine, two completely blank, two with the names Eddie

O'Kane and Joe Dan Touhy. The photographs of the two men were identical. When the photographer had said to the late Eddie Mavor 'smile,' he had failed to comply. So two frowning Mavors, under two different names, in two passports.

The time was now 10.45. By 11.52 Carter was back at the Yard, had processed the passports through the print section on the second floor and watched the police printers and photographers isolate two distinct sets of prints.

The next process took two hours—matching the prints. At 1.57 two names—Eddie Mavor, and a gent by the name of Joe Lear, photographer. 'Wedding Prints a Speciality', name spread over Yellow Pages (North), address Caledonian Road.

At 2.23 precisely Carter had got Mr Lear out of his bed by the simple expedient of continuously pressing the doorbell, whilst monotonously kicking the front door.

Mr Lear was an old timer and asked Carter outright for a search warrant, and Carter said that people who asked for search warrants usually had something to hide, and would he like to discuss this hypothesis at considerable length in the local nick. Lear demurred. Carter walked straight into the back of the shop, and found what he was looking for under a heap of rubbish in the darkroom. Another Irish passport, not blank, a different photograph, not Mavor, of a good-looking man going under the name Michael Mahoney. He had taken that back to the Yard arriving approximately at four am.

It was not until seven am that morning that the photograph of Michael Mahoney had been positively identified.

Lieutenant Ewing had nodded his agreement when shown it at eight am, and pointed out how close the photograph and expression were to the FBI photo.

The Irish Embassy in London supplied the information at

44

eight thirty am. They said that, seven months before, a batch of fifty blank passports had been stolen from Dublin Castle, and that the Provisional IRA was suspected.

At nine am Lieutenant Ewing and Inspector Jack Regan met again, but this time it was an official meeting. The two Irish passports found at Carlyle Buildings had belonged to Eddie Mavor. The photo in the Irish passport found in the darkroom of Joe Lear's photographer's shop had been positively identified by Lieutenant Ewing as the likeness of James Purcell.

Regan had been officially put on the Mavor case, which meant that he would be working with Lieutenant Ewing of the Frisco PD. The Mavor case and the Purcell case were now obviously part of one and the same investigation.

The first thing that Lieutenant Ewing said to his new partner, Regan, was that he was busy and could they meet later sometime? Regan said that was fine—he had plenty to do.

Ewing returned to the Bayswater Hotel, and asked the cabby to drive twice round the block where the hotel was situated. He was looking to see if SECURCOM had made the right noises in the right places. There were no parked cars with suspicious guys studying the hotel.

But it was early still—nine-forty-five am. It was raining.

He talked to the Hall Porter who lent him an *A to Z* of London and an AA map of England. He went up to his room, sat on his bed and opened the AA book. He looked up Wotton, Gloucestershire, where this guy Mavor was killed. He studied the route between London and Wotton, Gloucestershire. He reckoned it was a two and a half hour ride in a Jaguar. And the Hall Porter had told him it had arrived—a Jaguar 4.2 which the porter had managed to rent from a specialist car hire company in London.

After fifteen minutes with the map, he got up, strapped on his Navy Colt .45, took the street guide and the AA map down to the basement car park and found the Jag.

For the next half-hour he took a practice amble round London to familiarize himself again with a non-automatic car driven on the wrong side of the road.

He went back to the hotel and toured the block again, parked, and went into the hotel lobby. He came out and noticed there were two cars by the kerb opposite the hotel entrance.

He got into the Jaguar and drove off slowly. One of the cars started off slowly after him.

No, maybe he was wrong. Within half a mile the car had disappeared from his rear-view mirror.

He drove on another mile and the car was there again in his rear-view mirror. It was a red Alfa with two guys in it.

He drove through heavy traffic to Camden Town. Then he stopped and consulted the *A to Z*. Whenever he went to a town like LA, New York, Boston, and now London, he always went to the local left-wing bookstore and picked up their folksy mags. For the simple reason that they invariably had lists of where the action was in town—old movies, whore houses, demonstrations, theatre. Ewing liked all their crap.

He'd gone to the Compendium Bookshop, Camden Town, yesterday, and had seen an ad there for a Comic Mart in the Camden Town area today. He'd talked to a salesgirl who was too good-looking to be true. Compendium would be there with a stall at the Comic Mart; she would be manning the stall. Reason enough. He had taken down the address.

It was a large church hall, maybe two hundred feet long.

46

Ewing parked the Jaguar and waited. No red Alfa. He went inside.

A hundred trestle tables, and at least five hundred people. A lot of quiet-spoken beards and heavy-rimmed glasses, and a churchlike air except for the stallholders themselves who shouted cheerfully from one to another. Thousands upon thousands of comics, mainly American, but, as the British invented this illiterature, now turned kitsch, there were piles of *Beano, Dandy,* and *Radio Fun* which were unrecognizable to Ewing. Lieutenant Ewing had his own modest collection at home in Frisco. He had had a mother who'd doted on him until six years ago when she'd given up her personal fight against Richard Nixon, Mayor Alioto, and property taxes and quietly died. His mother had kept every toy and book he'd had as a child. It had shattered him when he'd found out that some pre-war editions of *Batman* comics were now worth half a grand apiece. He had some, and he was holding on to them.

He wandered through the push of devotees, looking at titles familiar and unfamiliar: *Godzilla, The Hulk, Jekyll and Hyde,* and *Frankenstein.* It struck him that there were hardly a dozen children in the crush. The average age of these curious people seemed to be around thirty, thirty-five.

He asked and got directed to the Compendium comics stall. The beautiful girl wasn't there. He was told she'd been and gone.

Meanwhile he was wandering the perimeter of the hall, looking out of the tall windows for a red Alfa. Suddenly it was there, parked in the street which was diagonal to the street where he had parked the Jaguar. The Alfa was empty.

This place is a mistake, he realized suddenly—too many folk. A bullet in the back of the head and the assassins melt into the crowd. He moved quickly now, pushing down the jammed aisles, aware of a number of faces that could belong to the driver and the passenger of the Alfa.

He passed straight out into the street, got into the Jaguar and drove off. They knew where they could get him. They would follow him back to the hotel. He would stage the meeting with them, or the collision with them, to be more advantageous to him next time. Next time being in the next couple of hours.

He drove back to his Bayswater hotel. The Alfa never appeared in his rear-view mirror. He took the maps out of the Jaguar and went up to his room again. He looked up Wotton once more, where the draftsman called Mavor had died. He started to memorize the route to Gloucester along the M4 motorway. He worked out distances and time, and decided that if the interception didn't take place earlier, he'd stop off for late lunch at Bath.

He took the maps and went back to the Jaguar. He drove south through the Park and right, along Cromwell Road, to Hammersmith. Then he took the Great West Road to the Hogarth roundabout. He had hardly got round the round-about when he saw the red Alfa, travelling half a mile to his rear.

Twenty minutes later he was passing the London Airport spur and they were still there, tucked into a pack of cars and trucks half a mile back. He guessed their objective must simply be to tail him, to find out where he was going. That suited him fine. His objective after driving them about for a few hours would be to corner them. Ewing took out the Navy Colt .45, slid it under the open map on the passenger seat, and relaxed. But his brain was ready to alert his right foot to hit the accelerator at a microsecond's notice.

The afternoon was cold and cheerless, with some light

rain. He turned on the car radio and tried the English stations before finding a distant Radio Luxembourg, with music that sounded like the Moody Blues strained through grit. Every ten seconds his eyes on the rear-view mirror.

The red Alfa stayed in the mirror. Once the car, bunched in the traffic, approached within a hundred yards, and Ewing got a closer look at them. They didn't look very Irish; more Sicilian—or maybe that was suggested by their dark complexions inside an Italian car. One was around forty and thin, with a long crop of black hair framing a sallow face. His companion was older. There were traces of grey in his hair and he had a thick moustache. They both wore dark suits. Whatever their business, they looked professionals.

It took him another hour and a half to get off the motorway and south to the city of Bath.

It was a place he'd always wanted to come to—the ancient Roman spa, wholly dominated by the yellowish stone Georgian squares and terraces. The flat, yellow-grey stone unique to Somerset and called Bath Stone.

He took the Jaguar round the two-mile, one-way city centre system, and selected, out of the half-dozen on offer on the George Street–Broad Street–Westgate circuit, the largest hotel: the Bath Regency Hotel. He'd worked out a plan. He went in and registered. Now the two men in the Alfa would presume he was going to stay there at least twenty-four hours.

He told the Hall Porter he'd be back with his luggage, went back out to the car, got in and drove north. Half a mile, trailing to his rear, the Alfa.

He crossed the M4 motorway again, passed Dodington House, and started to head for open country around Horton. To deal with the men in the Alfa he needed open country,

49

some hills, and maybe the two lakes described on the map as the Colmer Reservoir.

It was not at all difficult to pull off the switch. Past Horton he arrived at a small group of hills covered in a plantation of high pines. Three or four tracks switchbacked around the base of the hills. He pushed the Jaguar fast into a series of bends and intersections, and with the superior handling and speed of his car he lost them. Then he found the road that climbed up through the densest trees to the plateau top of one of the hills. He reached the top of this hill, drove the car in among some trees and braked. He got out, and climbed a fifty-yard slope to the pinnacle. From here he had a three-hundred-and-sixty-degree view over the countryside. For the next half an hour he saw and heard the Alfa backtracking and weaving around the intersecting tracks below. At one point it made a half-hearted attempt to climb up the mud-covered slope of the hillside towards the trees which concealed the Jaguar. The Alfa's tyres failed to grip the mud as the Jaguar's had. Finally it braked to a halt in an open area about half a mile south-west of Ewing's position. Obviously a debate was going on in the car. It lasted five minutes and then the Alfa took off, heading south. They were obviously heading back to Bath.

He went back to the Jaguar and started it up. He reversed it out of the trees and down. He'd achieved his purpose. They'd been following him; now he was following them.

They went straight to Bath, parked in a sidestreet next to the Bath Regency Hotel, and entered the hotel. Ewing parked the Jaguar in another sidestreet and carefully made his way to the street where the red Alfa was parked.

The first thing he saw as he examined the car was an air-carrier folder for a plane ticket lying on the glove tray under the facia. It was a folder for a BEA ticket. There was a name on the folder but he couldn't make it out. He moved on round the car, looked in the rear window and saw a briefcase tucked under the front seat. Below the briefcase handle, the initials TF. That was enough.

He walked down the street, found a side entrance to the hotel, and entered. Moving warily, he stepped into the lobby. The two men weren't there. He checked the dining-room and bar. They weren't there. He came back and crossed to the reception desk. The clerk looked up from a ledger.

'I'm still waiting for a friend who's bringing my luggage,' Ewing said.

'That's quite all right, sir,' the clerk responded.

'I wondered if you could tell me if Lord Dalhenny has arrived yet?' Ewing enquired.

'Lord Dalhenny?' The clerk looked puzzled, but impressed. 'We have no Lord Dalhenny staying with us at present, sir.'

'You sure? He said he'd be here by the time I arrived.'

'I assure you, sir, that Lord Dalhenny is not here.'

Ewing appeared to think about it. 'There's one possibility. He sometimes travels under a pseudonym—he's an important man in public affairs.'

The clerk nodded his knowledge of Ewing's fictional aristocrat.

'He goes under the name of George Hale, his first two Christian names.'

'I'll check the register, sir.'

'I think he also sometimes calls himself Carson, his mother's name.'

The clerk studied the register. 'There's no Hale or Carson here, sir.'

'Could I look at the book? I might recognize another name he's using.'

'Of course, sir.' The clerk turned the book for him to read.

Ewing's eyes went down the column of names to the last registration. The briefcase initial TF stood for Terence Feeny. Feeny gave a Camden Town address. The room number was 403.

Ewing had already been allotted Room 110. He now asked if there were rooms higher up in the hotel—the traffic in the square would make the lower room noisier. Was there perhaps a room on the fourth floor? The clerk checked and discovered Room 417.

The only risk now was that he would collide with the Alfa occupants on the way to the lift. He didn't. He went up to the fourth floor, and was shown into Room 417. He tipped the page-boy and returned almost immediately to the lobby. He bought a newspaper and retired to the furthest corner of the lobby, held the newspaper up to shield his face in the best tradition of spy fiction, and waited.

They came down for the set afternoon tea at three-thirty. They didn't see him. Now they were out of the car he could assess their physical capabilities. They were both tall and solidly made, younger than he was, and in good shape. They looked like a couple of bodyguards. He gave them ten minutes by his watch to go into the sitting-room and settle down to tea.

He took the lift back to the fourth floor, and entered his own room. He began to search for some kind of material that was stiff but pliable. He'd been on a recent SFPD refresher lecture on picking locks and entering rooms. The baldheaded captain with startlingly bad breath who had given the lecture had listed the best equipment for sliding a lock bolt back: the stiff cellophane sheet that stuck Gillette stainless steel blades to their display backing, the see-through cartons that toothbrushes are sold in. He had neither new blades nor toothbrush. He found a substitute. There was a plastic folder for the hotel services with pages inside listing tours, shops, and places of interest in the area. The loose pages were wrapped in a stiff plastic sheet. He didn't even have a penknife. He broke off a piece by bending it along an edge, back and forth a score of times. He then had a section three inches by one. He moved quickly out of the room.

The corridor was deserted. The cleaners would certainly be finished for the day and he would hear the sound of the lift well before it reached this floor. He moved down to Room 403.

It took two minutes to position the plastic sheet and start the bolt moving back. He heard the click, and the door unlocked. He listened for a moment. No sound from the lift. He entered the room.

The first thing he saw was the door to the adjoining room, open. The men had a suite. It took him ten minutes to do a thorough search and draw a blank. No notes, no scribbles on phone pads. Nothing.

He sat on a bed for the moment and had a think. Then he got up, pulled the phone as near to the door as its cord would allow, put it on the floor and went out, pulling the door to, but not closing it. He quickly returned to his own room. He was short of time. He calculated the minimum they would spend on tea was half an hour. He picked up the phone in his room and dialled Room 403. Then he dropped the phone on his bed and hurriedly made his way back to Room 403. He went to the ringing phone on the floor, picked it up and put it down on the bedside table. Then he took out a box of matches and broke a match in half. Holding one of the prongs of the phone in one hand he pressed the broken matchstick down the gap between the other prong and the plastic shell of the phone, jamming the prong solid in an upright position. Then very carefully, he replaced the receiver on the prongs. He had now manufactured a bugging device between his room and the room of Feeny and his companion. Everything they said would go through their telephone and be heard on his phone, up to the moment when they tried to make a call out. Then they would either discover the jammed prongs or think the phone had broken down. He walked out of Room 403 and closed the door.

They took an hour over afternoon tea. Ewing lay on his bed reading a *Country Life* that had been left in the room, phone cupped to his ear. He heard their door open and they came into their suite. They were arguing. Their voices were Southern Irish. Then the argument lapsed for a moment while they discussed what they were going to do. One suggested returning to London; the other said they must wait it out—obviously the Ewing feller would turn up. The other said he doubted it—Ewing had seen he was being followed and had given them the slip because he wanted to avoid them, and so wouldn't come back to the hotel.

'Then what in Christ is it?' the lower of the two voices demanded.

'I'm telling you, we phone Kavanagh and Parrish, then back to London—'

'I don't want to talk to the Broker. I don't want his advice about anything. I don't think he's a patriot. I don't trust him.'

There was a pause while the other man considered. Then he must have nodded, because the next noise Ewing heard was the sound of the door opening and closing. They had left the room.

He went to the door and waited for the sound of their footfalls down the corridor; then another pause and he heard the lift arriving, and the doors opening and closing.

Then he was out and sprinting past the lift for the emergency stairs at the bottom of the corridor.

He clattered down four badly lit flights of cement steps to the lobby level. Slowly he opened the door. His quarry had left the lift and was just disappearing out of the front door.

He had a problem. Their Alfa was parked closer to the hotel than his Jaguar. He had in fact to wait in the lobby as they headed out into the square and right, to the side-street and their car. It took off fast, back into the square, and east. It didn't worry him—he knew their destination. Nonetheless, as soon as the car had disappeared round the side of the hotel block, he was out and sprinting for the Jaguar.

The rain had gone. The day was brightening up. He felt relaxed behind the wheel, and fairly confident. The Colt was under his right arm, the Jaguar felt solid. He kept its speed within the legal limit, fifty miles an hour, which seemed fast in the narrow country lanes heading for the M4. He had just reached out to pick up his driving glasses from the seat beside him when he half glanced in the mirror and stiffened. The red Alfa was two hundred yards behind him and slowly gaining on him.

He saw signs for the approaching M4. He had to make the decision. He could out-accelerate them on the motorway. But point was not to escape them—he wanted to track them. He was confronted suddenly with the slip-road off to the left marked LONDON. He kept going, over the motor-way bridge, heading north and deeper into the Gloucester countryside. They were glued to his tail.

Three miles on, he saw a sign for the approaching village: HEFFINGTON; and another sign: NATIONAL TRUST, COLMER RESERVOIR, 1 MILE. His boot hit the floor and the Jaguar went through Heffington at ninety miles an hour, out the other side, and over the top of a hill as if the furies of hell were after it. Then he glimpsed the reservoir, two artificial lakes at the end of a long lane bordered by trees.

The first of the lakes was half a mile long. The second one lay a little beyond it. That was bigger, maybe twice as large, but darker and solitary, ringed in with a curtain of pinetrees that sloped up the hills on all sides. Ewing headed down the road for the second lake.

He found what he was looking for. The afforestation scheme around the lake was marked out by tracks off the road and irregular stretches of barbed wire in bad repair. Since the coming of the M4 motorway, this area would have less of the commuter driver passing through it, heading for Bristol. There were fewer strangers and tourists who were going to play with matches and start forest fires in the dense growth of young trees. Ewing decided to lose the Alfa in the forest. He turned off the dirt road which served as the lakeside route and accelerated through a break in the fence deep into the trees. He dropped the speed of the car to navigate in the gloom beneath the high branches. His concentration was still split between getting rid of the Alfa, wondering how they had turned the tables on him, and wanting to arrest and interrogate these two men. He moved down to the lake's edge and cut the pace right down.

Then he saw at the base of some pines half a mile up a rise in front of him the flash of red of the Alfa going fast. He braked. He saw the Alfa charge on, then brake, and the driver climb out and stand by the car. Ewing suddenly realized what they were up to. The Alfa driver had been driving faster than Ewing, then stopping his car every so often, switching off his engine, and listening for the sound and direction of Ewing's car. And he would hear the Jaguar engine because the sound of it was being reflected off the lake below. Ewing turned off his engine, then let the car roll slowly down a slight slope into some bushes.

He got out and moved to where he could see the other car. He couldn't see the men for a moment, then he heard the Alfa start up and he saw the driver coasting the car down to the lake edge.

Ewing's position now was half a mile from the red car and about a hundred yards above the lake shore. He could see what the driver was up to. There was a concrete pier which ran off the lake edge and out thirty yards into the lake, with some empty rowing boats and speed-boats moored to it. The driver cruised the Alfa down to the pier, up on to it, and drove to its end, where he parked. He and his passenger were obviously hoping to get a better vantage point of the whole of the lake shore. The driver got out, stood there for a few minutes, lit a cigarette, then climbed back in and wound down all the windows. If Ewing started his car, they would hear it.

Ewing deliberated. There were a number of unknown quantities about the situation. There was also the psychological element. It had been a shock to find himself the pursued, not the pursuer. He didn't like what had happened.

He started the Jaguar with a roar, slewed it out of the bushes, and accelerated with as much speed as he could get from the car downhill to the shore. He had a half-formed plan. He wanted to corner these men. Trap them. The idea was to drive up on to the narrow pier and block the Alfa's exit.

The Jaguar hit the sandy shore at eighty miles an hour, and slammed up the concrete ramp and on to the pier. He saw the men twitch round, anger and surprise on their faces, to find their prey bearing down on them. It was when Ewing saw the passenger reach down and try to bring up a sawn-off shotgun, and he remembered how the English crook Mavor died, that he changed his mind. He half braked the Jaguar and smashed it into the rear of the Alfa. The Italian car bulletted off the end of the pier and hit the lake surface with an explosion of spray. Ewing put the hand-brake on and jumped out of the Jag. He pulled out his Colt, ran to the edge of the pier, and looked down. He was in time to see the roof of the car sliding slowly and awkwardly below the surface.

He waited five minutes. Neither of the men surfaced. They were in that car and they were drowning, or had drowned—and alive they were valuable, and drowned they were useless and there was nothing that he or anybody else could do about it. And still he strode up and down, eyes searching the black water, and ten minutes passed, then fifteen minutes, and nothing came to the surface, except a slow, lazy oil-slick. 'Fuck!' he said finally, and very loud.

He went back to the Jaguar and studied it. The overhang in front of the car had been stove in about a foot, and the headlights broken. Otherwise the car was in driveable condition. He got in and pressed the starter. His hands were shaking, but in anger at himself. He knew that in this case leads were not going to come thick and fast. He had some names, those names he'd overheard on the bugged phone, Kavanagh and Parrish, and the Broker, who might be a third man, or a nickname for Parrish or Kavanagh. Two common Irish names and a nickname, and two dead men who sounded as if they could have been key witnesses. He'd blown it.

Meanwhile Jack Regan screwed himself at approximately four pm that afternoon.

Joe Arthur Harold Edward Thomas Lear was sixty-two years old and didn't amount to much more than the Christian names of his mother's five brothers and the surname of the man she reckoned was his father. Plus he was a lousy photographer and forger. He stood in more or less all he possessed, a shabby suit which had housed a wallet they'd taken away, containing thirty-two pounds in cash and one condom. The suit was grey, the boots were brown, the tie was blue, the hands trembling, and the face white. When Carter nicked him, he was squired to Notting Hill Gate, the nearest station to his photographer's shop. But the first thing that Regan wanted was for Lear to be brought to West End Central. There was some belief among the current gossip of the villains in London's underworld that West End Central was where they put the boot in while they asked their questions. And sometimes after the answers. It didn't happen to be true. Regan had seen no kicking done during interrogations at West End Central.

But the myth prevailed that West End Central was no place to hang about, and Lear, weighted by problems, one of which was guilt, plus five Christian names, was upset when they pulled him out of Notting Hill and shoved him into an interview room in West End Central and there was a Sweeney bloke there.

'Detective Inspector Regan, Flying Squad,' Regan said. 'Sit down.' Lear sat.

Regan changed his mind. 'Stand up.'

Lear stood up.

'Come here,' Regan gestured. He was standing by the window. He gestured Lear to join him at the window. 'Look.'

Lear looked out into London, or as much of it as he could see cluttering up Savile Row. People from another world parking their cars, heading off high-voiced to world-famous tailors, or West End restaurants with important names. Lear had never made it into one of those restaurants. Now he felt he never would.

'London,' Regan's finger sweeping across the visible horizon. 'There are nine million people out there. Did you know that?'

Lear nodded, but was confused by Regan's selection of that particular statistic.

'So why have we picked you to stick the Mavor murder on?'

Lear stood there and looked at Regan, blank and instantly shattered. It was obvious he'd never heard of Eddie Mavor. No quick shift of the expression at the name, just the eyes slowly opening wider and wider—amazement. He was on a murder charge, and he'd never heard the murdered man's name. He staggered over to the chair and sat down.

'Stand up,' Regan said quietly.

Lear lurched to his feet and stood there like a drunk squaddie on parade.

'First question, why—why did you kill him?' Regan asked, not too heavily.

'I don't know . . . who you're . . . talking about. . . .' Lear said it all in little gasps.

Regan sat down at the desk, opened and studied a file.

Sergeant Carter stepped into the room, closed the door

quietly, ignored Lear, nodded to Regan, walked across and took up a position leaning against the windowsill.

'Here.' Regan pulled the five Irish passports out from the file. He found the one with Purcell's photo in it which had been taken from Lear's shop, and opened the other four, the two blank ones and the two with photographs of Mavor.

He held up an open page of the passport with Mavor's grim look on a photo. 'You saying when you killed him you didn't know his name was Eddie Mavor? Distinctive enough name. You should've remembered it. You forged him two passports.'

'I didn't.' But this time, by Regan's calculation, Lear's voice carried less conviction.

Carter shifted his position at the window. He now leant his back against the high sill and folded his arms, eyes still on Regan.

'You were in Wotton Gloucestershire, four days ago, one-eighteen pm. You shot and murdered Eddie Mavor. I have two witnesses to prove it.'

'Bloody lies . . .' The old man, his head rocking forwards now, soft voice, almost in tears. 'Bloody lies . . .'

'Way I work, I ask questions before I formally charge you. I mean, for Christ's sake, you never know—we can always make it easier for you if you can make it easier for us. That's what we are, aren't we? Put a copper and a toe-rag caught on the hop together, you've got a couple of blokes who should make a deal.'

The old man wasn't listening. 'I need a glass of water.'

'Later.'

'Now. I need it.'

'Later.' Regan quiet but definite.

The old man's eyes filled with tears.

'You're the wrong side of a pension to go shooting people,' Regan said harshly. 'Especially people who are friends of mine. Especially such people.'

Tears and despair now in the old man's eyes.

'What did he do to you?'

'I've never met this bloke. . . .'

'That's your official line, is it?'

'Yes.' The old wet eyes on Regan.

'But you forged these two passports—your fingerprints on them. This is your form. You've committed every dirty little crime in the book. So why not in the twilight of your years, a new hobby for a retiring villain, murder? I mean, murder's what you're here for, forgery's a joke. But let's get that out of the way first. Did you or did you not in any way contribute to the forgery of these stolen blank Irish passports? Yes or no?'

The old man tried to clear his nasal passages and made a noise that Regan took to mean an affirmative. 'Good,' he said loud and clear, 'we're getting somewhere.'

He looked at Carter. Carter was doing the right thing. Just being a presence—a figure cold, impassive, saying nothing. He wondered vaguely how Carter would handle this; wade in, accuse an old man of murder just to shake him up? Probably not. Probably something subtler. On the other hand there was plenty of time for subtlety if the blitzkrieg approach didn't pan out.

'So the first time you met this friend of mine you murdered was when you took his photograph at the studio?'

'No.'

'Before?'

'I have never met him. I didn't take his passport photeys. I got give 'em. I just forged the passport, the stamps—'

'What stamps?' Regan asked quickly, wanting to get the man more and more committed to his forgery confession.

One admission of guilt obtained from a suspect and the ice is broken; more will follow, if there are more admissions to be made. He gave the old man one of the passports.

'Those ones, 'ere 'nd 'ere.' The old man pointed out the stamp which said: AMBASAID NA h-EIREANN, LONDAIN, and the die-stamp on the photograph. 'And I forged the signature.' He pointed out the signature of the consular official in London, a woman's name.

Regan, for a second, indecisive, not sure which way to go. But as soon as he asked the next question, he knew. 'You say you didn't take these photographs in your passport photograph studio. All right, who supplied them?'

It was just that second's flash of fear across the man's face, a fear that confirmed his belief from way back that he should never have taken this job and mixed with these people, a fear that it was better to be accused of murder than to point the finger towards them, which was certain death. They had told him that on three occasions, that he would die with two bullets in the back of his head if he ever said a word to the English police.

'The Dublin authorities say these passports were nicked by the IRA. Did they give them to you, and the photographs?' Regan's voice now rising. 'Did they give you the photograph for this passport which was in your shop?' He pulled the fifth passport out from under the file. 'This man? D'you know who this man is?' Regan's voice now sharper, harder. 'Do you know this man killed a policeman? Have you any idea how much trouble you're in?'

Joe Arthur Harold Edward Thomas Lear collapsed on the floor. His last gesture before unconsciousness was to try and pull a pill bottle out of his pocket.

It took twenty minutes to get a doctor to him, and fortunately the doctor identified the big pills as Adrinalex and

63

diagnosed that the man suffered from acute low blood pressure. They were the kind of pills you took every four hours. That's why he'd been asking Regan for water. The doctor opened Lear's mouth and pushed a pill down the back of it, and sluiced in some water. Fifteen minutes later, when the ambulance men got to the office, Lear was still unconscious. The police doctor directed Regan that he was not to attempt to question him for at least twelve hours. Lear was carried off to hospital. And Regan had blown it.

The Witches' Elm, Earl's Court Road, has three bars, graded by noise level. The public bar always jammed with Australians—Earl's Court Road having another name, Kangaroo Valley. In the public bar Antipodeans bawl at each other at such volume that the assumption can be made that they are to include within hearing range their bazzas and Sheilas in the Old Country. The middle level bar is the saloon bar, but Regan wouldn't go there because it was always full of the CID crowd from Kensington nick just up the road, and he knew them all, every constable, every sergeant and the four DIs. Regan went up two flights of stairs to a small purple wall-papered room called the Weigh-In Bar. The landlord had some association with boxing, and pictures of boxers, the sepia ones presumably long dead, the Kodachrome still alive and killing each other, adorned the walls. The forty-year-old barlady was repulsive. She even had a wart on the tip of her nose. She kept the place empty and tidy—which was how Regan liked it. He came to bars to drink and think. He did not understand social drinking. You either drink, which is a process whereby you get drunk, or you talk. The two operations as different as dying and gardening.

He said he would be there at eight o'clock. He joined Regan at one minute past eight.

'What's yours?' Regan asked.

'They have Jim Beam here?' Ewing's eyes going round the place.

'They would.'

'That's my shot.' Then he came to some conclusion about the Weigh-In Bar. 'This is not the finest pub in London.'

'If you don't like it,' Regan pretending that he was offended, 'we'll have one drink and go.'

'We'll have two drinks and go.'

They had three drinks—Regan on Bells, Ewing on Jim Beam. They were both consciously trying to relax. Ewing lit an American-brand cigar and studied Regan through the smoke. 'Right, how do we handle this?'

'Handle what?' Regan's voice deliberately vague, anticipating what was to come.

But it didn't come, not for at least another half a minute while Ewing adjusted the burn on his cigar with another match, and took a few sample puffs and found the cigar now properly alight and to his satisfaction. 'We're on the same case essentially. We work out the parameters, who does what. . . .'

Regan could sense the game and play it that way or any way, any time. And he did and he took his time, and a few sips of his Bells. Then he looked up at the American. 'Superintendent Maynon, Mr Haskins, Carter, you. Everybody's decided we're on the same case.' He lifted his glass and swallowed the whisky down. 'I haven't.'

'That a fact?' the American said. 'So what the hell are we doing sitting here?' In Ewing's eyes the hint of anger; Regan was getting to him.

'Because Haskins or Maynon can order me to work with you, and I think it's a good idea for the two of us to get together so I can convince you it would be a lousy idea. Like when I move on a case I move fast. There's no time for explanations to a fucking tourist.'

Ewing's eyes suddenly cooled. He understood now that Regan was being deliberately intimidating, and he wasn't going to be intimidated. 'Okay, that's the way you want it —fine,' he said off-hand. 'It strikes me, like it'd strike most people, we're going to be covering the same ground.'

'When did I say I'd conceal information I uncover from you? All I'm saying is that the brilliant ideas you have about solving this case wouldn't interest me.'

'And that's the end of this pub crawl?' Ewing asked flatly.

'Jesus Christ, man! You misunderstand completely. It's the *start* of this pub crawl and a reasonable working relationship.'

Len drove them on to the Red Lion, opposite South Kensington Tube Station. Regan bought the drinks. Ewing found a quiet corner in the saloon bar.

'Married?' Regan wanted to see whether Ewing would produce one of his profound pauses before an answer.

Ewing didn't. He answered directly. 'Not now. Two divorces.'

'Kids?'

'No.' After that the pause. Ewing wasn't going to reciprocate the questions.

'Allow me to tell you the gripping saga of my sex life,' Regan said, just loud enough for the two barmaids to shift uncomfortably. 'Married a female hustler and divorced her more or less on the same day six years ago. Adorable eight-year-old daughter whom I see probably five times per annum but weep frequently and guiltily over, and probably will do so later tonight. At the moment I'm banging a German ex-*au pair* girl who fell on me two years ago. We lay on long weekends when she moves into my flat. I rarely see her at other times. It kind of doesn't work, if you see what I mean . . . ?'

'Uh huh,' Ewing said. It was obvious that nothing that Regan was saying interested him.

Over the next two hours they covered six pubs. It was the first time Ewing had been driven by Regan's driver.

'You know you're the only police group in the world that—'

Regan cut across. 'The Metropolitan Flying Squad is the only police unit in the world where each man, be he a sergeant or superintendent, is driven around by chauffeur just like Aristotle Onassis. Tourist-copper talk. Concentrate on how we're going to drink ourselves to death tonight. Would you like to go south of the river?'

For the next few hours Len shipped them from one pub to another, eight in all, the length and breadth of London. Regan was officially on duty, officially on the Mavor case. He had to log some movement for the night.

Regan was getting drunk and watching Ewing get drunk. It was an interesting performance. The man got quieter, more reflective, gentler as he tanked up. Regan was watching Ewing because he was waiting for something. The American had been missing all day. What had he been up to and where?

Ewing had already decided not to tell the British police about the men in the red Alfa at the bottom of Colmer Reservoir. Or not to tell them yet. The guys were beyond producing information. The police procedure of any country would involve him in at least one wasted day while the

67

car was recovered, the bodies identified, the questions asked, and the reports written. And there was always the possibility of something funny happening with these English guys—like sticking a manslaughter charge on him. He was satisfied that his action had been justified. One of the partners in the Alfa had pulled a shotgun on him and presumably would have used it had Ewing given him another second.

On his way back to London he'd realized that the bigger problem he'd have that day would be the Jaguar, with the front end now stove in. It was the Head Porter at the Bayswater House Hotel who had booked it, but as soon as Ewing dropped the man a twenty note there was suddenly no problem.

'The car hire company is insured, sir.' The man had said as he palmed the twenty pounds off the reception desk.

'But here's my problem. I want another Jaguar, delivered here within a couple of hours. Because I'm checking out.' Ewing had then put another twenty on the desk.

'Give me your Diner's Club card again, sir. We'll have another Jaguar here within two hours, sir.'

They had delivered the new Jaguar half an hour later, at seven-thirty pm. Ewing had driven it to his new hotel, the Mount Park Hotel, Bayswater Road.

He had decided to change hotels because SECURCOM, in spreading the word in the crime ghettos in London, had produced the goods—the two guys in the Alfa. Now these two men had disappeared, the Bayswater House Hotel might become a pressure point. He could maybe organize SECURCOM to help out with his personal security while he stayed there. But he had now thought of another use for the SECURCOM company.

Regan came back from the bar and stuck a glass down in front of Ewing. 'Old Grandad. They have no Jim Beam.'

'Fine.'

'All right Lieutenant Ewing, what have you been up to all day?'

'I changed hotels. Mount Park Hotel, Bayswater Road.'

'What else?'

'I cruised around waiting for your group to come up with something. Like you say, I'm just a fucking tourist.'

Regan searched the American's expression as he lied, and wondered why he'd lied, and began to realize that he wanted to find out. But it would take patient hours to get anything out of the Yank. 'Pubs are closing. One more. I'm tired. I'm drunk.'

'I've got a few questions to ask you.'

'Fuck your questions. One more drink.'

'Fuck you,' the American said gently. 'The night is young. And I've yet to meet your beautiful German girl friend. . . .'

Regan's flat in Hammersmith had once belonged to his mother. She died seven years ago—the year of his divorce. Regan was five foot ten. His mother had been a little woman. The flat was a little flat, four little rooms full of little things—little coffee tables, little frames with small pictures in them. A little kitchen with little teacups, and a living-room with a little sofa, and a bedroom with a little bed. The flat came complete with a little Spanish maid who cleaned it once a week. The one cleaning was enough because Regan was hardly ever at home. The only two things that Regan had done to change the flat were to throw out his mother's bed and to move in a large Dunlopillo king

69

size one and a rota of girls to go with it. That was until two years ago, when he had met Tanya Moller, then aged twenty-six.

She had been a witness to a robbery. She had been outside a bank, just walking in, when two guys came out. She had been able to describe them in great detail. Regan had never met anyone quite so observant. From the moment he met her he wanted her and eventually she reciprocated. And he was flattered and gratified. That changed after the first wild romantic and sexual month. They had found they were two people who loved each other but just couldn't live together.

Then they both hit on the idea of weekends. The fact was he was too busy and involved with the job—that's what had broken up his first marriage. She moved out of the *au pair* world and became a secretary to a German goods importer in London. Her work was well paid but exhausting. So she would be there on Friday night whatever time he got in, and they would screw maybe a couple of times and then they would talk, or rather she would talk, until dawn. And Saturday she would go shopping, get her hair done, meet girlfriends, and she would return Saturday night until Sunday at nine pm. But usually he would be working Saturday night well into the small hours of Sunday morning. And he'd come back to his flat and she'd be asleep and sexually satisfied from the previous night and he would be wide awake still from the adrenalin of excitement or fear from some job he'd been out on and he'd sit in the little chair by the bed and look at her face on the pillow—her blond hair spilled across her face in sleep—and wonder what the hell their relationship was about.

It wasn't always just weekends. There were periods when he'd been assigned to an important investigation that was

70

in its early stages, just ticking over, and he could see that tomorrow night or the next night he'd be free—and he'd phone her up and she might also be free. That would happen maybe once a month, rarely more.

The time was eleven-thirty and the manager of the Cherry Bush pub in Battersea was quite insistent that Regan and Ewing and four other drunks should go. But Regan was almost finished telling Ewing the details of his organized sex life with Tanya, and how beautiful she was, when Ewing made some remark like when exactly was he going to get the opportunity to confirm this. So Regan staggered to his feet and went over to a coinbox phone, brushed the landlord's protestations aside, and called Tanya and told her to come from her place to his flat in Hammersmith for a drink and to meet an American. She said no. He said in that case he would come over to her flat and ring every bell on the entry phone—and there were twenty of them—and wake up the whole bloody building, because he wanted to see her. And he'd thought about it and he wanted to talk to her about some Very Important Things. And she could tell that he was drunk and capable of ringing every bell in the block, so she agreed to go to Hammersmith.

The sharp spring night outside the Cherry Bush hit Regan and Ewing in different ways. Cold air made Regan more drunk; possibly because he was more tired. The same air sobered Ewing up. He had still the residual effect of being on San Francisco time, eight hours behind. So four days ago this particular time would have been mid-afternoon.

By the time Len dropped them off at Hammersmith, Ewing was sober, Regan drunk, yawning, fumbling his keys, and having problems wrestling with the manual lift-doors.

She opened the door and she was beautiful and coldly

71

furious. She weighed up the situation in a glance. That Regan was very drunk, and a row about his threat to wake up her entire block of flats would be wasted. But that his companion looked sober.

'My name's John Ewing,' he said gently.

She nodded. 'Tanya Moller.'

'Coffee, where's the coffee?' Regan had already blundered past them into the kitchen.

She turned. 'The coffee is made and is in the sitting room and I suggest you have some immediately.' She turned back to Ewing. 'May I take your coat?'

'I won't be staying long.'

'Stay.' It was a double-edged invitation. Her expression implied the missing reason. It was 'stay because I'll need help with this drunk.' Meanwhile she was also looking him over, and approving him. 'Jack seems very drunk.' It was a statement rather than a question.

'He's had a hard day.'

'That is nothing unusual.' She had taken his coat and hung it on a hatstand, but she still stood in the hall, as if reluctant to go to the living room and sort out Regan.

'He's on a case he doesn't want. I'm also on it. He has to carry me.'

'I'm sure you would be a help rather than a hindrance to him. Come and have coffee.'

The coffee didn't sober Regan up. It mellowed him a bit. The three of them sat there. No one seemed to have a subject for conversation. 'What kind of coffee is this?' Regan asked at one point. 'It tastes like cats' piss.'

'It's decaffeinated coffee. I've found where to get the decaffeinated beans.' She turned to Ewing. 'Like Sanka. The coffee does not keep you awake.'

She wanted to draw him into the conversation but he was

all politeness—silence. She interpreted this at first as his inability to cope with drunken Regan. Then she realized that he wouldn't find any problem in dealing with Regan, but he was quiet because he was studying her.

A point arrived about twenty minutes later when even Regan began to notice his own yawns. He turned to Tanya. 'I think it's bedtime.'

'I'm not staying here tonight,' Tanya said. 'I have to get up early in the morning. I haven't brought my night stuff.'

Regan looked angry.

Ewing downed his second coffee and stood up. 'Which way are you going?'

'I live behind Marble Arch,' she said.

'I live on Bayswater Road. We'll share a cab,' the American said.

'You didn't bring your night things,' Regan suddenly said loudly, as if he'd just registered it. 'Why the fuck d'you need your night things to stay here?'

'Jack Regan, you should go to bed,' Ewing said heavily.

'I'm alright,' Regan snapped back. 'I've decided to stay up all night. . . .'

'You're alright, but I'm not. I'm tired. Your girl's tired. So we'll go off.'

Regan nodded. 'Right, you just do that. Get out. I'll see you tomorrow.'

Ewing picked up his coat and followed Tanya to the door. Regan's head already slumped on to his shoulders and he was asleep. Ewing opened the door for Tanya, and they walked out.

It took them twenty minutes to find a cab, then another twenty minutes to cross night London and arrive at a little block of service flats off Bayswater Road.

73

'Thank you for dropping me off. It was nice to meet you, Mr Ewing,' Tanya said.

'I remember telling you my name was John.'

The back of the stationary taxi was dark and they were parked under a fused street light. She could not make out his face or his expression. 'I hope we meet again, John.'

'Your boyfriend Jack says you spend weekends with him.'

'Is that what he says?' her voice quietly annoyed. To have arrived at a statement like that they must have been discussing her sexually.

'So give me your phone number. Your weekends are with Jack. That leaves five other days.'

She wanted to see his face. His voice was so firm, assured. She felt like telling the cabman to switch on the inside lights. The man was obviously making a direct sexual invitation to her including an explicit betrayal of her lover, and she wanted to see if there was a smirk on his face. In that case she would ridicule him. She laid a silent bet that the expression, if she saw it, would be honest. Ewing had weighed up the situation of Regan's two days a week and considered that there was nothing very sacrosanct about that relationship.

And as she thought about it that way she faced the reality of her recent relationship probably for the first time.

'There is no light to write anything. The surname is Moller, Tanya Moller. The address here is Melbury House, W 2. You'll find me in the telephone book. And I would like you to ring me.'

James Purcell sat in the Assistant Vice President's waiting room of the New York Bank and Trust Company, 300 Eastcheap, London EC 3, and studied his notes and his correspondence like an actor having a last look at his lines before the first-night curtain went up.

This was an important performance. It wasn't that he didn't have most of the information to plan the robbery, it was that he had to check on some critical pieces of information. Check, simple checks—but to do those he'd have, at this interview, to erect a tissue of lies so complex that the Assistant Vice President would be so overwhelmed and so confused he'd start to let vital clues out.

And if he didn't, then, so far, James Purcell had committed no crime in England. He could fly away and shrug it off.

That's the deal he had made with the IRA Provos and the man they called the Broker. He'd said: 'I hope to pull this bastard off. I promise you nothing.'

And the Broker had said: 'Sure,' just like that. The IRA Provos were one of the most experienced bank-heist outfits in the world. They knew the problems.

After the meeting with the Assistant Vice President he'd have some idea of the scale of the problem. On the surface the thing looked so good there were moments when he couldn't believe it.

And it had looked good two weeks ago and three thousand miles away. Cousin Michael had called him, and he'd gone to New York. Michael, an extremely distant cousin from some almost forgotten link on Purcell's father's side, did a lot of things for his living and nothing legal. He was twenty-four and was into a number of causes besides financial self-improvement. One of those causes was fund raising in New York for the IRA. Cousin Michael had been born in Dublin, Ireland, although his parents had emigrated to the US when he was four. He had discovered Irish Nationalism at the age of twenty-two.

Cousin Michael had a few grey hairs from knocking over a bank on his own, aged nineteen. The grey hairs now had a black rinse. Purcell reckoned that Cousin Michael was surely the only New York IRA fund raiser who was a practising homosexual.

The meeting had taken place in the black-leather apartment of a reconstituted duplex in Cornelia Street, Greenwich Village. Cousin Michael knew that cousin James had done stir on a drafting job, in a Memphis jail, when he'd never been within a hundred miles of the raided bank. 'My friends need help,' Cousin Michael had said. 'What makes them my friends is they pay.'

The first things Michael's friends had paid for were some airline tickets.

They had flown to San Francisco, Purcell, Michael, and two large guys who had talked little and had given out only their Christian names. In a small neat house in a Frisco suburb they had met a small neat Pole called Karminski.

Karminski was fifty years of age, broody and bitter. He had just been fired after twenty years with a leading West Coast Bank Security Installation company. Purcell and Michael had to sit through two hours of loud emotional recrimination. Purcell couldn't work out whether the guy had been fired because he was untrustworthy or whether he was honest up to the second he was fired, and then had grabbed for anything he could get.

What the Pole had got was a lot of information about security devices in a lot of banks in the US and elsewhere. He was selling, and had already sold, bits of this information to various interested parties in the Underworld. Cousin Michael wanted to know about the London banks—the Pole had gone to London at some point and installed

American security devices in some American banks in London.

The Pole had two items for sale. One was the master list of main safe combinations for these various London banks he had worked on. When a security device installation man works on a safe the first thing he has to know is the combination of the safe. The Pole had kept a record of these combinations.

Cousin Michael told the Pole that he wasn't interested in acquiring the combinations of some London bank safes. Combinations of bank safes are usually useless because most modern bank safes have a time lock. They can be opened only at preset times and always during the regular day trading hours of the bank. A combination is only useful if a gang is going to do a daylight raid. It was not Cousin Michael's or Purcell's intention to do a daylight raid.

The Pole kept returning to the subject of his instant dismissal from the company he had served so faithfully for so many years. Michael cut straight across the tirade. 'How much d'you want for the complete security installation plan of the New York Bank and Trust Company, 300 Eastcheap, London?'

At first the little Pole wouldn't put a price on it. Then he said fifty thousand dollars, and Cousin Michael laughed —a hollow, nervous, dangerous sound.

The Pole said quickly that he was open to discussion about it. So the three of them went out and had a long drunken dinner, followed by an hour in a hostess club, with the little guy getting more emotional and maudlin and finally breaking down in tears in the men's room.

Meanwhile the two guys with Christian names only, who had flown with Purcell and Michael from New York, were burgling the little wall safe behind the refrigerator in the

Pole's house. They got the safe open. They packed all the papers in it into a briefcase and took a cab downtown to an outfit called Multicopy All Nite Xerox. Within a quarter of an hour they had a Xerox of the entire paperwork in the safe including the bank safe combinations and floor plans of the security installations at New York Bank and Trust Company, Eastcheap, London. They took the Pole's papers back to the safe, locked them up again, and left the little house as scrupulously neat and clean as they had found it. The Pole would never know he had been burgled.

At 2 am Michael and Purcell had delivered the man back to his home. The little guy was besotted with drink and woe, and about to pass out. He mumbled and burbled his final decision. For the floor plans and the safe combination of the London bank he would not take less than twenty-five thousand dollars.

'Fuck off,' Cousin Michael had said gently, as he turned and hailed a passing cab. He and Purcell got into the cab. They did not look back.

The little Pole sat down on the pavement outside his house and tried to staunch the flood of tears that came, with his two hands pressed into his eyes.

Purcell had started the job in New York. Michael had siphoned enough cash through from his sources to finance the setting up of an office, installing a telex, printing and forgery of essential papers. For several weeks Purcell had worked on the drafting, writing his notes, redrawing the wiring diagrams, making discreet calls to fellow experts in circuitry, walking the wind-sharp streets of springtime New York, puzzling over the plan again and again—was it just stupidly ambitious, or was it possible, a raid of these dimensions, a heist of historic proportions? He knew that no

78

one in history had ever tried anything as complex as this before. For three weeks he puzzled and worried and wrote and drew and then he made his decision; it was possible. The concept could work. It would now be down to assembling the right personnel to pull it off.

'Mr Kreinhof will now see you, sir.' Mr Kreinhof's secretary, a tall woman with a Brooklyn accent as stiff as the Bridge, gestured Purcell towards the Assistant Vice President's office.

Mr Kreinhof turned out to be a small man with a serious look. He extended a dumpy hand. 'Of course, I've heard all about you from Head Office, Mr Karolyi.'

Mr Kreinhof had not heard all about Purcell, now Karolyi, from Head Office at Number 17, Wall Street, New York. He had received a letter with a forged signature purporting to come from Head Office, New York. 'What can I do for you?' Mr Kreinhof sat down behind a desk too large for him, and spread his hands as if he could offer Purcell the world for the asking.

'The letter from your Head Office presumably explained that I am Vice President of Security Aid Corporation of New York, and your company has suggested that I come here and discuss with you the subject of increasing your security situation in this bank. How it can be done. And why it should be done.' Immediately Purcell produced from a bulging briefcase a large bunch of expensive leather-bound sales aids. Purcell bundled them on to Kreinhof's desk, knowing Kreinhof would be too busy to read and assimilate them all. Therefore, psychologically, he'd want the thing explained. It was just from talking to him that Purcell would get the answers he needed. Purcell started the patter. What Security Aids was selling was a complete new look at the phrase 'security in depth.' Two minutes into the chat Kreinhof was out of his depth.

'Mr Kreinhof, there is a new kind of criminal about us. We've seen 'em back home, the Germans have them in Germany—the Bader Meinhofs—the French have them in France, the Ulster Government in Ireland. We call them political criminals. They're young men and women, vicious thugs, some with Ph.D.'s in physics or chemistry or philosophy, who have rejected our social system and are out to destroy it. And they rob banks, Mr Kreinhof. And they rob them cleverly. That is one of the things these people do. . . .'

Kreinhof nodding, but very vaguely.

'One of the problems in detecting these people and bringing them to justice is they are frequently many more times intelligent than the forces of law and order whom we entrust to hunt them.'

Kreinhof nodding.

He's not a stupid man. He looks bright. He's just a little slow, Purcell decided. 'Now, they know how to rob banks because essentially all bank security is minor variations on the same theme. Touch-pads, photo-electric systems, electrically timed openings of safes, carbon steel fittings, security patrols, etcetera. These people can look at a bank and guess exactly where a touch-pad is, where, in a floor or ceiling, the cables for re-circuiting alarm systems are likely to be hidden. These people are bright. Our company, Security Aid Corporation, takes their knowledge away from them. Every bank premises where we have remade the security system is unique and different from any other bank. And the bonus of our system is you retain your original security system. Our system is overlaid, a completely separate double check on your system. That is why your Wall Street office has sent me to see you. I think they believe the next place for politically motivated bank robberies is London.'

Kreinhof now surprised and concerned.

'Yes, Mr Kreinhof. That's what your Head Office believes.' Purcell lit a cigarette. 'First off I have to say that my presence here, sent by your Head Office, is obviously a matter of secrecy and security. You'll note the letter I bring from your Vice President, Mr Goldberg, gives you a special telex number for all communications between yourself and Mr Goldberg about my work here. When you check the telex number you'll find it belongs to a new subsidiary of New York Bank and Trust Company, namely New York Trust Security Incorporated, Suite 505, Number 197 Wall Street. You should write or telex any queries about my activities to Goldberg at that address, and not to Head Office. In this day and age, the enemy has so often proved to be within. . . .'

He talked on with Mr Kreinhof for another half an hour. At the end of it he had quite enough information to rob the New York Bank and Trust Company. He had, in fact, enough information to rob a dozen banks in London.

They picked Purcell up in the Roof Top Bar of the Hilton Hotel—Paddy, the Curzon House Hotel waiter, and the thick-necked hard case who had chauffeured them on the previous occasion. Paddy had an altercation with the *maître d'* entering the Roof Top Bar, probably the last bar in England where a tie is required to drink scotch. The *maître d'* came into the bar to select Purcell from Paddy's description. Purcell came out. Paddy said one obscene word to the *maître d'*. The *maître d'* said nothing.

They drove straight to the Broker's house in Brent.

As soon as the bell was touched, the Broker opened the door. He ushered them into the hall. Paddy and the hard case disappeared off into a side room. The Broker conducted Purcell through the dark house to the comfortably furnished room at the back.

'I didn't introduce myself last time. My name is James Kavanagh.' He did not extend his hand, but gestured Purcell to a seat. 'Also I didn't tell you why they call me the Broker.'

Purcell said nothing. He was aware of movement, and low voices, towards the front of the house. The doorbell rang. More soft voices. The sound of the front door closing.

'I'm Irish, but I wasn't involved, until recently, in Irish politics. I was a "broker". That's the name over here for a person who finds, or puts up the money to finance a particular crime. I'm a professional, unlike these patriots.' He thumbed towards the front of the house. 'It's worth bearing in mind, Mr Purcell, that I am a professional.'

Purcell didn't understand if the man was trying to convey some unmentionable subtlety in the explanation. He'd think about that later.

Purcell wondered about the other people in the house, the doorbell ringing again, more voices, other doors opening and closing.

'How did it go at the bank?' Kavanagh asked.

'I'll give you some points. It would take hours to explain everything. . . .'

'The salient points, Mr Purcell. . .'

'I guessed right, no London clearing banks have preset time controls on the opening of their safes. It's expensive equipment. London banks have limited robbery insurance. I think they take the risk.'

The Broker was nodding, as if all this was news to him, which it probably wasn't.

'The set-up for American banks in London is totally different. The reason is that the safes of American banks in

82

London are repositories of stock certificates, mainly convertible, held by US citizens and firms in this country. These stocks are worth millions. It's these stocks, and cash in sterling and dollars, we're going to steal.'

Purcell talked on as if he had given this lecture several times. 'Because of the large amounts in these safes, and because English insurance companies require special precautions to protect these safes, the London American banks have imported American-manufactured safe-security equipment. I've seen the New York Bank and Trust Company's safe. My assay of the situation is it's like stealing candy from a kid.'

The Broker sat back and looked thoughtful.

'The timing mechanism on the safe. I met this guy in San Francisco who had worked on the installation of safes in London. The safes have a time-clock on them where, even if you know their combinations, they cannot be opened except between the hours of say, nine am to five pm on five weekdays, when there are people constantly in the bank.'

The Broker was slowly nodding.

'That's why they have this crazy night and weekend security patrol, by this firm based in South Audley Street.'

'But you're saying the combinations are useless unless we make it an office-hour daylight raid; we wouldn't be interested in that.'

'I'm not saying that. On the side of these safes is the Bulova electric clock that times the opening and closing. This is a complicated business to explain, but the principle is simple. We're going to get a Bulova clock to open the safe in the middle of the night. There's a fail-safe device in America where if you tamper with this clock, the safe jams up permanently until Bulova come and sort it out.'

'I see,' the Broker said. He didn't.

'However, in installing this equipment in England, and in

adapting it from 120 volts AC to 230 volts AC and inserting a step-up transformer, they have had to cut this fail-safe device out. D'you know how an electric clock is powered by the AC cycle?'

The Broker shrugged. 'No.'

'Suffice it to say, I've been down the Tottenham Court Road, bought a soldering iron, solder, bits and pieces of electrical equipment, and I've made a box of tricks which I will cut into the Bulova clock circuit. Then it'll take a minute for the hands on that clock to spin round an hour. And that safe will be ready to be opened not at nine am but at three am or any other time we decide.'

There was a long pause while the Broker studied him. Then he stood up. 'Come with me.' Formal now, alert. It was an order.

He led Purcell out of the room and down the corridor, and left, into the front room of the house. In the front room there were fifteen men sitting in chairs around the walls deep in some discussion. The Broker led Purcell to the middle of the room. All eyes were on him. Purcell had an uncomfortable feeling, a prize bull in the auction ring, these farmers, calculating his worth at stud, or slaughter.

'Our new draftsman. He calls himself a number of names —Kalman, Purcell, Christopher, Thompson. . .' The Broker said flatly.

Purcell wondered about how much power the Broker wielded with these people. Would the Broker end up one day like their last draftsman—would he, Purcell, end up like their last draftsman.

The Broker was introducing the fifteen people. 'Parrish, McEvoy, Declan Murray, Murphy, Traynor, Martin,' rolled off in an anti-clockwise direction—all big men. They were the bulls. Purcell had his first inkling of the real possibility of

84

danger developing on what he'd assumed would be a down-the-line operation. He nodded, and the names nodded to him. But at the end of the circle of introductions his eyes came back to meet the eyes of the only man that the Broker had given a Christian name to—Declan Murray. There was something about Declan Murray that would worry anyone, including Purcell. His height, the granite cold quality of his eyes. He was the only one who had not nodded, or acknowledged, the Broker's introduction.

It was just that. A circle of introductions, then the Broker was leading him out of the room and opening the front door. He pointed to Paddy the waiter, and the silent chauffeur in the car at the kerb. 'Paddy will take you back to the hotel.'

Purcell faced the Broker. 'I don't think that was a good idea security-wise. Introductions, exchanges of names. The less we know about each other the better.'

The Broker pursed his lips, calculating the simplest way to express it. 'I wasn't introducing them to you. I was showing you to them. For the purposes of identification, do you see? If you ever play games with us, Mr Purcell, there are fifteen men who know exactly what you look like, when they come to kill you.'

Noon. Regan got into the car and Len drove to the East End. Carter had, as usual, not only done his routine research last night and this morning, but had come up with other things besides. Carlyle Buildings, Jamaica Road, SE1, like many other slum blocks of flats in London, was owned by the Commissioners of the Church of England. The lease for Number 14 was in the name George Smith—so obviously a pseudonym for some villain that Carter had checked at Tower Bridge, the local nick. The CID there had never heard of a George Smith of Carlyle Buildings. While he was about it, Carter asked the nick if they knew of any honest citizens in Carlyle Buildings who might give the Sweeney a lift up and advice. It took Tower Bridge CID two hours to come up with one name. There was a bloke worked nights on the Corporation road-washers—He'd been helpful with some honest news on a villain some time back. He might be bent now, but he was straight nine months ago. His name was Davies, address, 31 Carlyle Buildings.

Regan climbed the stairs to the top outside corridor of one of the two blocks which comprised Carlyle Buildings, and pushed down through the lines of damp washing to the extreme end to check whether, from the Davies flat, the ubiquitous Mr Smith's front door on Number 14 in the adjoining block could be seen. It could.

He rang the doorbell. There was no one in the open-curtained front room, but from the back of the flat the sound of theme music from a lunchtime TV programme. He waited half a minute and rang the bell again. Night worker, waking up, watching telly in bed—Regan decided as a possibility, as he rang the doorbell for the third time. There was the sound of shuffling slippers and a bronchial cough. 'Who is it?' A woman's voice.

'Police,' Regan said.

'What d'you want?'

'Open up, please, missus.'

A door-bolt snapped back and the woman, aged around fifty, appeared in a nightgown.

'What d'you want?' she repeated.

'I wonder if you or your husband can help us in a certain inquiry.'

'What inquiry?' She yawned in Regan's face.

Regan took a half a step back as the stale breath hit him.

A man's voice bellowed out, drowning the TV at the back of the flat. 'Who is it, love?'

'Police,' 'love' answered.

'Old Bill, local nick?' the male voice enquired.

'Sweeney,' Regan answered loud.

'Jesus Christ, why didn't you say?' A second later a slight, stooping man appeared, naked from the waist up, zipping up his trousers. 'What d'you want, Mister? What does the Sweeney want with us?'

'Help with some information. From the end of this balcony you can see Number Fourteen. I wonder if you can tell me anything about it? Whether you can describe any person you might have seen entering or leaving it?'

The man knew nothing; the woman knew too much. Or she knew a certain amount and talked too much. She knew that flat belonged to an Irishman; she didn't know his name. She hadn't seen him for a long time. She had seen other men using it. How many? Well, actually, one. She gave an accurate enough description of a man who wasn't Mavor. The man had a lot of crumpet, birds. How many? Three. What did they look like? More accuracy now—a woman describing women. Expensive clothes, girls who had their own cars. Call girls probably, from the West End, slumming it with a hard case, with a hard one, down the East End. Two blondes described, then to the *pièce de résistance*, a full description of the third girl—tall, flash, heavy in jewellery, spade. 'Real slag tart, hair frizz up like a Woolworth mop. A proper darkie, like Africa. Not your West Indian. Some of them West Indians aren't so bad when you get to know 'em. But this one a real sambo. And I arsk you, what is Africans doing in England? I mean when were our lot in Africa larst, with colonies?'

Regan shrugging off the historical enquiry, looking for something that was a positive lead, but in a way the psychology of the situation was to let her run on, while her old man went back and got his shirt on. Regan inhaled the stale breath of British Fascist working-class bigotry, and, when phrases had been repeated once too many times, he shot the question. 'You don't know how I could get in touch with the blackie—like you haven't told me, when did you last see her here?'

'Week ago.'

'And you've no idea how I could get a hold of her?'

'Course I know how to get hold of her. She's a stripper down the Jockey Club, Jamaica Road. Her black tits are on photeys all over the bloody front of it. School kids can see them. My old man says that's all right 'cos it teaches kids what gell coons are for, but I think it's bleeding daft— bloody Jockey Club's right next door to the Baptist Church. . . . Hey, do you want. . . ? Hey, I haven't finished. . . !'

Regan was pushing his way back to the staircase through the lines of washing.

The Jockey Club, Jamaica Road—Regan tried to remember how many other names it had gone under, and how many managements had actually gone under. It was a post-war building which stood on a corner site junction of Jamaica Road with Ellesley Road, and near the High Street. So there was a lot of passing traffic about and people about. Regan told Len to cruise the car round the block twice, because he'd noticed something.

'I remember it as the Park Lane Suite, Skylight Club, the Penthouse. Then those thieving Cypriots took it over and it became the Famagusta Club, and the Hellenicana and God knows what else,' Len offered.

Regan working it out, not failing to notice what the lady

88

in Carlyle Buildings had pointed out—the big tits on photos in the club entrance and the spiel: 'Martha de Amour—She Sings, She Strips. Ten More Beautiful Girls, Continuous Nitely . . .' Other lovelies in other photos, all spades. Audience presumably a spade audience.

'Notice, Len?' Regan asked at the beginning of Len's third tour round the block.

Len nodding. 'At this time of day, the club's not open. They're not bouncers. . . .'

'What?'

'Bodyguards, guv?'

Regan nodded slowly. There was a front entrance, and there was a side entrance to the Jockey Club. The man idling at the open doors at the front of the club was over six foot, massively built, a bullet head and a pink face, and a tiny cigar jammed into the teeth in the middle of it. To the side of the club his companion was, if anything, larger, certainly heavier, and very dark, probably African. 'I wonder if there's another entrance to the club. Left. Then pull into the kerb.'

Len turned the Vauxhall VX 4/90 left and out of sight of the heavy at the side door of the club, and pulled the car into the kerb.

'How long do I give you, guv?' Len worried, knowing that Regan was going to go past the two goons to find out who or what they were guarding. And concerned about Regan's chances *vis-à-vis* the height and width of the goons.

Regan didn't answer. He studied the ten-foot-high brick wall of the rear of the club. 'Take the car up on to the kerb, along the wall. I'll use the car roof as a leg up.'

Len eased the car up on to the kerb and slid it alongside the wall.

A minute later, Regan was out of the car, eyeing up and

down the back lane, then up on to the car roof, and a leap and a grab and he was on top of the brick wall. He got a leg over the wall and changed position, so that he was facing the wall again as he dropped on to the hard cement of the backyard of the club. He fell the wrong way. Pain detonated up from his right ankle. He spent the next minute gasping and cursing as quietly as he could as he hobbled in circles around the dustbins full of waste food and empty bottles that littered the yard.

He put his weight down on the ankle and it seemed all right. He stepped through the rubbish and over to the yard door. His hand went out to grasp the handle. It didn't because the handle was yanked open inwards with the door, and Regan realized two things very quickly. One, that there was obviously a burglar system, probably touch-pads, in the yard. And secondly, that the man who had been standing guard at the side door of the club was the largest black man in the world.

It wasn't just his height, it was his mass, his confidence, his obvious fitness. The black man was grinning. Regan was already consigned to some amusing part of his memory where he stored details of people he threw back over ten-foot walls they'd dropped from.

'Detective Inspector Regan, Flying Squad,' Regan tried for openers. It was apparent that this was not the subtlest approach.

The black man took out a cigarette, lit it, still grinning. 'The warrant to enter these premises?'

Regan thought about that. Thought about the whole spectrum and possibilities of negotiating with the big black grin, and meanwhile listened to the music, the girl's voice, and the piano, both tinkling out from somewhere in the building.

'You need a warrant to search a premises, friend, not to enter it.'

That gave the African something to think about, while he changed position edging out of the door trying to look behind Regan, still grinning, maybe thinking there were others out there whom he would be tossing back over the wall.

Regan stepped past him.

A huge hand shot out and grabbed Regan by the shoulder, a vice grip, rooting him to the spot. Regan was stopped and stopped himself. He looked into the grin. 'That's technical assault.'

The grin widened. 'Why be technical about it—you want a real kicking?'

'I'm looking for Miss Martha de Amour.'

'Not any more.' The big man began to gently haul in on the grip and the shoulder pad of Regan's overcoat.

Regan jabbed a right fist fast and hard on to the man's nose. He saw the pain jerk every muscle across the face. That was less than a second of observation because both of Regan's hands went up and grabbed the man's hair and jerked down in that moment of automatic reaction when the black man's hands moved too late to protect his face. Regan's knee came up as he pulled the man's head down. The hands couldn't protect the nose again. The force of the knee hit the nose a second time. Regan knew the effect, as calculable as the simplest equation—two steam-hammer blows to the nose unplugs the tear ducts, blinds the eyes with tears. Next move, always spin a big man on his axis—own weight will not aid him unless his feet are solidly placed. Regan kicked hard at the big man's ankle as he straightened, blinded. He kicked him, angling his foot so that the part of the shoe that connected was the solid inside edge of the heel. The black man tipped over twenty degrees while still trying to straighten and grab blindly at Regan.

Regan's hands went back to the man's hair, pulled him right round, accelerating a body that was already stumbling over bottles and more rubbish to the point where it must fall. A final thrust on Regan's part to place the exact area where the top of the black man's head should connect with the brick side-wall. Then the sound of the skull concussing as it smashed into the wall. And the black man was out for the count. And as inert as any of the other rubbish in the yard.

Regan picked up the black man's cigarette, still alight, broke it in half, threw away the filter end that the man's mouth had touched, and inhaled once on the remaining half. He made his way over to the door and stepped into the rear exit from the club.

She looked better than her photographs. She was one of those girls—they exist—who look worse after a hair-do. Sitting on a bar stool pulled over to the piano, she was not made-up and her hair was flat down. And it all added up to a good argument against Max Factor and Vidal Sassoon, or any other argument at all.

A little white pouf about five foot high was her accompanist. As Regan approached her she studied him and somehow she got better looking. But there was pain on the little guy's face, because she was not a good singer and the pouf was the only one in the world who cared about this. Except Regan, who allowed her to finish. The lyric was about a girl who comes from the country to the big city to get a job in a house as a maid, and it turns out she has other duties. The song was accompanied by obscene gestures—presumably part of the strip routine. Regan was interested that she would go to the trouble of rehearsing with the pouf to get the song right. A Jamaica Road audience pays for the sight, not the sound.

The song ended. She dismissed the pouf with a slight sideways movement of her head. They both knew instinctively what Regan did for a living. The pouf glowered at him, and disappeared off through a curtain at the back of the stage of the low-ceilinged room.

Martha de Amour moved gracefully across the floor and around behind the bar and pulled out a diet American Dry and spun off the top. 'I suppose you don't drink on duty?' she announced.

'I drink scotch on duty,' Regan corrected.

She found a glass and a bottle of scotch and slid them across the bar top to him. 'I have a large friend, sits around the yard outside. He makes sure no one troubles me. He's tall and dark and . . .' She didn't continue the description.

Regan poured himself a large scotch. 'I met him.'

'He's supposed to make sure I'm not bothered by anyone.'

Regan sipped the scotch and thought about it. 'We came to an arrangement,' he said.

'Which leaves another good friend of mine out front,' she said gently.

Regan nodded slowly. 'Yep. Somebody wants you protected.'

She smiled. It was an open smile. 'Did you like my song?'

'You want me to be honest?'

She nodded.

He pursed his lips as if really thinking about it. 'I think you should work on it.'

She nodded.

'Not here.' He finished the scotch. 'Why don't we go to

your place and sing me a song about a girl who comes from the country to be a maid in a big house and ends up with more bodyguards than Fidel Castro.'

She smiled brittley. 'Fidel Castro the cigar millionaire?'

'The same.'

'Actually I don't have time. Busy day for me. Maybe next year.'

Regan decided she was intelligent, attractive, bright, and as hard as a rock. 'Madam, the person who has least time is me. This your handbag?'

It was not anybody else's. It was sitting on top of a fur coat on a bar stool. Regan snapped it open and upended the contents on the bar.

'Hey!' she shouted. Her expression changed to fury. She made a sudden move left, obviously aware that the only functioning bodyguard was the baldheaded lumberjack out front.

Regan's right arm grabbed and hauled in on her wrist. 'Madam. Sit down!' His voice suddenly cold. She thought about how he must have tamed the gorilla in the backyard, and sat down.

'Your real name Martha Williams?' There were two letters in the handbag with the name and an address in Kensington.

She shrugged the question off.

'Okay.' He gathered the contents back into her handbag, handed her fur coat over the counter, and kept her bag. 'Side entrance. Don't wake the dog at the front.'

She came to the instant conclusion not to resist. In fact she steered him to the side entrance to the club.

They came out of the club and made a left turn and headed down and round to the back of the block. Regan put her in beside Len. He got in the back of the car.

'Fifteen Blenhurst Mansions, Campden Hill.' He'd got the address from the two letters addressed to Martha Williams.

'Right, guv.'

Regan relaxed in the back seat, wondering where this was going to lead, feeling gloomy, not feeling at all positive about anything that was happening in this case. Then suddenly, and he was almost startled by the sound, he heard crying. Miss Martha de Amour Williams was crying. It was obvious from one look at her face and her trembling hands that she was crying from fear.

Detective Sergeant Carter and another detective sergeant colleague of his arrived at five-fifteen. Lieutenant Ewing arrived about quarter of an hour later. Regan wanted as many as possible; he wanted 15 Blenhurst Mansions, in the luxury Campden Hill sector of Notting Hill Gate, taken to pieces from ceiling to floor.

Martha Williams sat it out on a hard-back chair placed dead centre of the room. She looked miserable. Regan refused her a phone call to a lawyer from the phone in her own apartment on the grounds that he wasn't yet arresting her, and although she knew he was not legally entitled to do any such thing, she would reserve the remnants of her resistance for refusing to say anything at all.

'Anything specific that we're looking for?' Ewing asked. He'd been there ten minutes, poking around, wandering from room to room. It was a five-roomed flat, beautifully furnished, with views across the gardens at Campden Hill and on to the high tree-line of Holland Park beyond rooftops a quarter of a mile away.

'There's the same feel about this place as Carlyle Buildings, right?' Regan surveyed the activity, Carter and the other detective sergeant pushing the furniture around, moving a coffee table to get access to a cupboard. 'Carlyle Buildings a slum, this luxurious. One thing in common, both set up for instant flight. This place isn't lived in, it's camped in.' He turned to the girl. 'Right?'

She said nothing.

Carter paused from his exertions. 'If it's a camp site, guv, what the hell are we taking it to pieces for?'

Ewing answered for Regan. 'We have no other leads.' He turned to Regan as if what he'd said had reminded him of something. 'I want to talk to you.' He indicated the door to the empty dining room. He wanted to talk to Regan alone.

They went into the dining room and Ewing pushed the door shut. He moved thoughtfully over to the window and looked out over the trees. 'What the fuck are we doing?'

Regan had been waiting for some such question. He had sensed that Ewing was disturbed about something.

'I'll tell you what we're doing. We're into something, the Mavor case. You know, we could spend the next ten years checking out the last twelve months of a small criminal.'

'So?'

'The Mavor case produces Carlyle Buildings, produces this black girl. Maybe you're solving the Mavor case. I'm not solving the Purcell case.'

'They're the same.'

'Maybe that's the mistake.' The American thoughtful, concentrating. 'I'm beginning to believe they're not the same case—the connection's remote. Purcell is in England as a draftsman to plan some kind of robbery. What robbery, why Purcell? That's my investigation. Now, if you can definitely link Mavor, the black broad, Carlyle Buildings and here, to Purcell, fine. Otherwise we have to go our separate ways, right?'

Regan didn't have to say anything. He was an experienced cop—he didn't even have to nod his agreement.

Carter found the letter. He and the other detective sergeant had moved on from the living room into the bathroom.

The cabinets were empty; the girl's basic make-up was still packed in a travelling case. There was a paperback on top of a laundry basket by the lavatory. It was an Agatha Christie —*The 4.15 from Paddington*. Carter had opened it and the letter had fallen out.

It was one page and a photograph. The page was unsigned, but it had a date on it. It had been written a week before. The photograph was of a tall, good-looking, forty-year-old man in Bermuda shorts and a floral shirt, standing in the sun outside a large building that looked like a hotel. Carter took it to Regan. Regan studied the photo and handed it to Ewing. Ewing shook his head. It wasn't Purcell.

' "Dear Martha, I have to stay away for a bit—say two months until things cool down. Don't go screwing around. Wait for me. It's sunny here in France and I need the rest. Two months is not a long time to wait. . . ." ' Regan quoted aloud from the letter, held it up in front of Martha. 'Who?' he asked.

She turned her head aside.

'If he's nobody we won't bother him. If he's someone important we'll identify the photo soon enough.'

No answer.

'Where was the letter posted from?' Regan pushing the photograph up in front of her nose.

Ewing's hand came out and took the photograph. He studied it. 'That looks a helluva lot like the Hotel Negresco, Nice. There's bound to be a photo of it somewhere in a travel brochure.'

'Except the photograph doesn't mean he's staying at the hotel,' Regan returned.

'Maybe the girl knows that.'

Regan shrugged. The girl wasn't going to talk, yet. She

was frightened, confused, and all that would come of a state like that would be a stack of lies. 'Carter, see Detective Inspector McCarthy, Bomb Squad. He's in charge of a photo file on IRA. Take this.'

Carter took the photo of the man and went. Regan, Ewing and the other sergeant continued the search. Ewing going through a cupboard of clothes, duplicating Regan's search of the same cupboard and the same clothes, men's clothes. There were a couple of suits, two drawers of laundered shirts, a drawer of socks and ties. The bloke's clothes hung up tidily. Martha's clothes laid out, hung up behind doors, as if she had never moved in. Martha sitting there, alternating silence with quiet weeping.

After an hour Carter phoned back. The man in the photograph had been positively identified by the Bomb Squad as John Declan Murray, Operations Chief of the Provisional IRA in England, now believed to be abroad.

At six-thirty pm, the Secretary of the Maudsley Hospital allowed Regan, with Ewing in tow, an interview with Joe Arthur Harold Edward Thomas Lear. 'Not more than five minutes, and the Matron will be present and will signal you to leave if she thinks your questions upset the man unduly.'

Lear looked well on the way to recovery—both his health and composure. Regan took less than five minutes. He held the photo of John Declan Murray, Operations Chief of the Provisional IRA in England, up to Lear's nose. 'If you identify the man in this picture as the man who gave you the passport photographs of Purcell, and asked you to forge the Irish passport, you're no longer on a murder charge. Is this the man who gave you the passport photos of Purcell?'

Regan didn't want an actual admission, he wanted the

knowledge; Ewing wanted a direct link between Mavor, Purcell, and the IRA provos.

The look in Lear's eyes told them the answer was affirmative: Murray had brought him Purcell's photo. Then, after a pause, Lear nodded his head, looked frightened again, and turned his face to the wall. Regan and Ewing walked out.

Two o'clock in the morning the phone rang in Regan's flat. He was in a half-sleep. He considered the alternatives of answering it or not. It couldn't be anything else but Squad Office at the Yard with either a real or imagined crisis. If the news was really crisis news then the night switchboard sergeant would be instructed to ring his number every quarter of an hour until it was answered. But he'd kept them waiting on previous occasions. If the phone rang off and then rang back in fifteen minutes from now when he would have had the chance to wake up properly, then he'd know it was Squad Office. He groaned—he was now awake from debating with himself the possibilities. He picked up the phone.

'I woke you up?' That was the question, but Ewing didn't wait for an answer. 'I got to talk to you. Out loud,' he added, 'you understand?'

'Talk,' Regan grunted. He didn't understand.

'I went to bed at midnight. I usually sleep well,' Ewing's voice contemplative, as if he was settling into some long story. 'But I got to thinking about things, you know?'

Regan didn't know.

'Something happened today. And it was at that black girl's apartment in Notting Hill Gate. Something wasn't right.' Ewing lapsed into silence.

Regan could almost hear Ewing's mind calculating some unidentified imponderable. 'What?' he asked.

'You know what I mean by hunch, gut feeling?'

'I know 'em. What d'you mean?'

'Something happened at that apartment while we were there today and I don't know what, but I have to go back to that apartment now, and see over it again.'

'Now?'

'And that's why I haven't slept.'

'Now?' Regan's voice sceptical. At the same time he was interested. He knew that, if Ewing had a hunch or an instinct about something, it would be worth following up.

'How do I get in there? Do I need a search warrant?'

'That's academic as Martha's in our custody. But I don't think we ask her for the front door key.'

'Okay. Who picks who up?' Ewing asked.

'You pick me up. I have to wake up.'

Twenty minutes later Ewing arrived.

'I'm awake,' Regan announced, climbing into the Jaguar, and pointing out the way east to Campden Hill.

'And you want an explanation and I haven't got it. I saw something at that apartment this afternoon. I don't know what I saw. That's it.'

Regan studied the American's face in the half-light reflections from street lamps. Two-thirty now in the morning —still some traffic motoring in isolation on Kensington High Street. Ewing's face a mask. Regan wondered how much of Ewing's talent as a detective was based on instinct. He'd assumed the guy was a textbook cop, like his own immediate superior, Haskins, like too many of them. Regan thought about that, worked on it, and realized that he knew as much now about Ewing as he knew four days ago when he met him at London Airport, and that was nothing.

At 15 Blenhurst Mansions, Campden Hill, Ewing rang the doorbell several times. No answer. John Declan Murray, Operations Chief of the IRA Provos and Williams' hump, was not answering or not there. Regan picked the lock. He'd brought along his little leather pouch which some burglar had left behind after fleeing the scene of a crime years ago.

'What d'you think we're looking for? What do I do?' He stood with Ewing in the centre of the living-room. Ewing didn't answer. Eyes vague, he wandered into the kitchen.

'Why don't you make us some coffee, Jack?'

Regan annoyed. 'You brought me along to make coffee?'

'Make coffee, don't make coffee. . . .'

Regan made coffee, set a cup down for Ewing on top of a portable television, then followed him round, sipping on his own cup. Ewing was going over the apartment systematically again, stripping the beds, searching drawers, checking out the bathroom cabinet, Martha's unpacked bag of make-up, the man's clothes, presumably John Declan Murray's. Ewing even studied the tins of food in the kitchen cupboard. He completed his search. He hadn't found the mysterious something he was looking for. He started again. He got about halfway into the search. Then he turned to Regan. 'You took the letter and the photograph that came from Murray in the South of France? Where is it?'

Regan took out his wallet and opened it and handed over the photograph and the single sheet of airmail paper.

'You keep evidence like this in your wallet?' Ewing asked. It was a criticism.

'Sometimes I keep evidence in my jock-strap; frequently I lose it. You ask around. They'll tell you—dear old Jack, always losing key documents. . . .' Regan sat down, now suddenly tired, knowing the American had failed to deliver the goods. By the time he got home to Hammersmith he'd have lost most of a night's sleep. He didn't mind losing a night's sleep providing there was a good reason. Ewing had obviously drawn a blank.

Ewing read the letter aloud. ' "Dear Martha, I have to stay away for a bit—say two months until things cool down. Don't go screwing around, wait for me. It's sunny here. . . ." ' '

Regan looked at his watch. 'You need me? Why don't we continue this tomorrow?'

Ewing ignored him. Regan could see his eyes scanning the letter, the photograph, re-reading the letter, studying the photograph again. And then Ewing's eyes stopped on the photograph, and his head swung round to the bedroom. And he was off pacing into the bedroom. Regan was on his feet and following him.

'Jesus, we're blind bastards.' Ewing pulled open the cupboard that housed Declan Murray's clothes. He pulled out the drawer which was packed with Murray's shirts in cellophane laundry bags, and up-ended it on to the bed. The shirts spilled over the bed. 'How could we miss it?'

'Miss what?' Regan clueless, getting annoyed with Ewing.

'The photo. We're supposed to believe the photo was taken recently in the South of France, and we're to believe the letter that says he ain't coming back to England till two months from now. The photograph wasn't taken recently—maybe it was taken years ago. Or maybe it was taken recently but the guy flew back immediately. But I don't think his girl knows. I reckon she's decided he's abroad for two months.'

'What the hell are you on about?'

'This beach shirt.' Ewing picked it up off the bed. Now he'd drawn attention to it, Regan suddenly understood.

The beach shirt in the laundry cellophane was a neutral gray print on a light yellow background. What was printed on the material were the letters of the alphabet, but small print. It took close inspection to see the little-print alphabet.

It was the same shirt that Declan Murray was wearing in the photo outside the French hotel.

'He could have two of the same shirt?'

'No. You buy identical formal shirts. You don't buy identical beach shirts. You buy different kinds, different fun patterns.' Ewing went out of the room, and came back with the coffee, now nearly cold. He sat down on the edge of the bed and took a sip. 'My proposition is that this guy Declan Murray, who relates to Mavor, whose occupation relates to Purcell, was not in France a week ago posing for this snap—and then staying on for two more months, meanwhile sending his shirt back airmail to be laundered and stuck in that drawer.'

'What's your proposition?'

'He's told his girl friend he's gone missing for two months. He's arranged for an old photograph to be sent from the South of France, to her, and to anybody who might pick her up—us.'

'Well?'

'I don't know what Purcell thinks he's got himself into—I'd say organizing this photo and letter to be sent, these arrangements, smell too elaborate a groundwork for a simple bank robbery. . . .'

Regan walked into Flying Squad Office at nine am. Ewing was already there. Detective Sergeant Carter walked in a second afterwards and said that Haskins had been in at eight and would be back at ten and wanted a charge, something to stick on her, otherwise Martha Williams must be released.

'Then find something.' Regan addressed his Sergeant sharply. He'd had three hours' sleep and he was irritable.

Sergeant Carter had spent six hours last night, and two

hours this morning, trying to find something. Anything—a parking ticket summons unanswered, a Hire Purchase debt.

'There is nothing on Martha Williams,' Carter said, and he walked out.

Ewing turned. He had been standing looking out of the window. 'What the hell do you want her in custody for. We want her out of custody when we question her.'

Regan's expression showed that he didn't follow the reasoning.

'That girl is a tough broad. She isn't going to talk unless she's persuaded. And that's better done in privacy.'

Regan's eyes hard on Ewing's. 'I'm sorry, Lieutenant Ewing, you'll have to spell that out for me. . . .'

Ewing didn't answer immediately. The silence got heavier in the room. 'Martha Williams has to talk. Your Sergeant Carter says there's no holding charge. So she gets released from West End Central. I'll be there. Give me a few hours.'

Regan sat down behind his desk. The logic was infallible. Martha Williams was a stripper with a background in crime. Under normal interrogation she'd take days, maybe weeks, to come across. He doubted Ewing would have to put too much pressure on the girl. Just walking into her apartment, and a couple of shoves and threats would do it.

Ewing didn't give him time to think about it. 'I'll be in touch.'

The tall American walked to the door. 'By the way, I got to tell you something. You're going to find out. It should be from me. I was with Tanya last night. . . .'

Regan's jaw dropped. There was a full twenty seconds of astonished silence. 'What the fuck d'you mean?'

'I mean I don't believe in deception. I am telling you I screwed your girl. And if you want to do something about it, you'll do it to me, and not to her.'

Regan couldn't believe it, the suddenness of it. Apart from anything else it didn't add up. 'You were with me in Williams' flat most of the night.'

'I said I couldn't sleep. I lay and stared at the goddam flower wallpaper on Tanya's ceiling, and I phoned you at two and I left her and went to your place.'

There was nothing that Regan could think of to say.

The tall American's untroubled eyes were on him. Then he turned and paced out of the room.

They walked in Hyde Park. It was the kind of morning that London weather can only conjure up half a dozen days in any spring. Eleven am, warm, almost hot. And bright sunlight charging around the park, touching up all the colours, and breaking open the buds of wild primroses under the trees.

The warmth in the air was kind of mockery. Regan studied her. Her expression as cold as her words. But he wasn't blaming her. He also wasn't blaming himself—he was blaming no one. And he cared about her and Ewing, and yet didn't care. And he certainly didn't want to know the details. But she had told him, as if it was an explanation, that the guy had taken her home the night Regan got drunk. He'd phoned her the next day, had come round at about eight and taken her out for an hour's dinner in some lousy local restaurant—so bad that they hadn't stayed for coffee. And so she'd suggested back to her flat for coffee.

She hadn't heard from Ewing today. Obviously she had assumed that Ewing would tell Regan what had happened at some point, but not within hours.

And Regan listened to her trying to make little bits of excuses knit together, and sounding so obvious and honest as she talked on, but his thoughts were ranging elsewhere. It had been the most serious affair since his marriage broke up. Some of the phrases she was using now were the same pay-off lines that Kate had used six years ago to pull the curtains on that second-rate drama.

Tanya talked, but Regan was recalling another voice. Chief Inspector Pirie Taylor, probably the only man who had ever meant anything to him on Squad. Taylor was a man of forty-five who looked sixty. He had a face that had been lived in at least three times. Taylor worked alone, lived alone, drank alone. He had died in a POLAC on the M1 chasing some bugger for no good reason. The squad car had blown out on the front offside tyre and had gone into a bridge upright. Taylor had commented to young, newly married, Detective Sergeant Regan: 'Why did you get married, son? What the hell have you got to offer a woman? Except "maybe" ? Maybe be home tonight, maybe see you tomorrow night, maybe see the kids, maybe take a holiday. Women are social animals. They need a man around. If you stay in Flying Squad, you're not available.'

The story of his marriage and now the story from Tanya's lips; Pirie Taylor would have smiled. Tanya was saying: 'For instance, why did you not phone me and take me for the meal John took me to? You two are on the same case. Why did he have time to call and take me out, and not you? I mean the reason's obvious.'

'What?' He asked mildly: 'You're not that daft to think I've got another girl?'

'No.' She protested with a kind of hopeless shrug. 'The opposite. You don't even have the time John Ewing found for me. You certainly don't have time for two women. Except maybe the famous seven minutes with a tart. And you would be studying your watch.'

She'd worked the whole thing out. Now his role was apparently to listen and maybe at the end agree to split, or stay together. He didn't know.

'I've asked you a specific question—will you answer? Why, if you and John Ewing are on the same case, sharing the same work equally, could he have time to take me out, and not you?'

'I went to bed, ten o'clock, to try catch up some sleep.'

'John Ewing didn't.'

'I know he didn't. He was banging you.'

Her eyes flashing anger. 'I don't think that's funny.' She snapped it out.

He was nodding. 'I don't think it's funny, either. I'll tell you something—and this I think is where it all goes wrong. I thought that you cared, not loved, cared. Enough for me to have a certain confidence in you. The confidence, say, to take a night off, get some sleep. That's a possible definition of love —confidence. And when that's gone, the whole thing, the lousy house of cards that everybody lives in, caves in. . . .'

She wasn't following his words and he knew it wasn't her English or lack of it, it was her decision.

'And I know something else. You screwed Ewing to get at me. You knew you'd failed to make me want you enough to elbow the job. But you always looked for the test. Then the perfect one. Two blokes, equal billing, on the same case. Why could John Ewing phone you up and not me? Answer? Because you're a whore. And that makes it a lot easier for me to forget you. I've known a lot of whores in my life. I've forgotten every bloody one of them.'

She stopped walking and talking. Her eyes started to fill with tears. They'd reached the Marble Arch gate. Twenty yards away he saw an empty cab in the traffic. He signalled the driver. The driver saluted back. He left her standing by a flower bed and walked to the cab without a backward glance.

110

'I hit her twice. Once on the side of the head. Once on the jaw,' Ewing said the moment he opened the door at 15 Blenhurst Mansions.

Regan stepped past him.

'Here, wait.'

Regan could hear a low moan coming from the bedroom. He halted and turned.

'She delivered the goods,' Ewing said gently, as if it justified and dismissed his action.

'Goods?'

'Like she really thinks her boyfriend's abroad but she's come up with an address of a farm north of Bath. She says all his IRA pals stay there.'

'You think that's the truth?'

'I am confident that she decided to tell me the truth.'

She was sitting hunched up on the bed, moaning into a Kleenex—about the tenth Kleenex she'd used. The rest were on the floor by her feet, each soaked in blood. The white nylon eiderdown on the top of the bed stained every square foot with some smear of blood. Regan wasn't shocked because of that. He'd seen, in his experience, people lose more than a pint of blood from a split lip. He was shocked by the calculated callousness of it.

She looked up. She remembered him as the Squad Detective from the night-club interview. 'You fucking shit-head,' she said, a blood trickle on her lips. 'How could you let this maniac loose, you fucking Sweeney bastard . . . ?'

Regan turned to Ewing and lifted an index finger, gesturing the American to follow him out into the hall. Once out of sight of the girl, Regan turned and steam-hammered his right fist round to hit Ewing in the solar plexus. The blow never connected. Ewing's right arm came across, and his body slid sideways and Regan was spinning, his blow fended off and reduced to total ineffectuality.

Regan was amazed by the speed of the big American's reaction. He stood there. It was obviously pointless to throw a second punch.

'What was that about?' Ewing said softly.

Regan took his time to answer. 'You hit the spade too hard. That wasn't the agreement. You fucked my love life—a whore called Tanya—that wasn't the arrangement.' But he didn't know where the hell to take it from there. 'What's the address of the farm?'

'Islade Farm, Hamnett, near Bath,' the American's cold eyes on Regan, his fingertips touching the area of his jacket sleeve where he'd fended Regan's blow.

'We take the spade down to Notting Hill nick, charge her —I don't like the irony—with assaulting you in your civilian capacity as a fucking tourist. You probably have a slight bruise on your arm from brushing off my blow. . . .' Regan turned back to head into the bedroom and collect Martha.

Ewing's hand came down on his shoulder and Regan spun round expecting the punch. But Ewing just stood there. He took a few moments to carefully phrase the words. 'I have to warn you,' he said quietly. 'Don't ever try to hit me again for any reason. Don't ever lay a hand on me. Understood?'

'The need won't arise,' Regan said hard. 'The next time you piss me about I'll get a gun and blow your fucking head off!'

'They're not getting on,' DCI Haskins told Superintendent Maynon. 'Not at all well, I'm delighted to say.'

They were in Maynon's office. Maynon was cleaning out his pipe with a penknife and wire brush, the thorough, once a month overhaul. 'Roger, you're skating around. What are you saying about Ewing's usefulness reference Regan? And would you say it in words of one syllable.'

Haskins took a moment considering the simplest way. 'I think we can make Regan obey orders, be part of a team, discipline him, teach him a permanent lesson, through the agency of this Yank.'

'How?'

'We've made them partners. I think it'll be an unholy partnership, and make appalling mistakes. If the mistakes are appalling enough, we boot Regan out of Flying Squad. If not, we threaten him with endless disciplinary action unless he settles and stops the general cavalier behaviour which has become his stock in trade. Ewing is the catalyst for breaking Regan down into useful and manageable components.'

Maynon began to fill his pipe. His expression as he digested Haskins' ideas seemed unsure. 'We'll have to wait and see.'

Regan and Ewing walked into the conference at one pm. By then there were about twenty men in Maynon's office. Regan sat down and his eyes went round the faces. Most of them he knew well, some were just vaguely familiar. This type of meeting happened often enough but there was always that slight shock when an investigation suddenly threw up something, and in came the heavy brigade. Regan and Ewing had been quietly investigating a dead snout, and some vague connections with West Coast, USA, and they had been setting their own pace. Now an address of a farm north of Bath had turned up that could be HQ for the leader of the IRA provos in England. Suddenly a lot of large grim men crowding into this office. Regan knew that this meeting was going to be a fifteen-round heavyweight wrestling competition and the prize was the case, and the challenger was the

Bomb Squad, and the title at the moment was held by the Flying Squad. But that meant nothing.

Maynon stood up behind his desk. 'There's a DCI in Bath and Wells CID. Name of Minshaw. Worked under me for years here at Squad. One hundred per cent reliable. I've talked to him. He's gone to this farm address to keep an eye on it. If there's any kind of exodus before your operation, he'll call in his CID lot.'

A disapproving sound coming from a large baldheaded man—DCI Patchin, Bomb Squad. Patchin now leant forward and started to voice his doubts. 'Guvnor, I'm deeply disturbed about this. Declan Murray and his associates are obviously and exclusively our province, certainly to the extent that we carry their files and have had, for three months now, a warrant for Murray's arrest. We're delighted your people have turned up this address. Assuming this farmhouse is some sort of centre, and terrorists are holing out there— I'm sorry, but we were first on the Murray case. It will, of course, be our province to plan raid strategy.'

Maynon said nothing. Patchin's argument was basically sound if Bomb Squad had opened the case file on Murray first and had a warrant out. Maynon was waiting for somebody else to disagree with Patchin.

Regan studied Haskins. There was a pecking order. Haskins as Squad DCI should answer DCI Patchin. But Haskins was sitting there looking sour, as if he'd been deprived of breakfast this morning and now, because of the timing of this meeting, was going to lose his lunch.

Regan waded in. 'I have some observations, sir.'

Maynon nodded.

'I'd say if one were to characterize our work on the Flying Squad, it's gathering information and carrying out raids. Equally I'd characterize the Bomb Squad as very good people

114

who rush around searching Left Luggage Offices and organizing the military to unknit gelignite from alarm clocks. Or who are very good at TV interviews when the bombs have gone off before the Bomb Squad got to them.'

He could see the colour begin to rise on Patchin's neck. 'What the fuck are you talking about, Regan?' Patchin's voice hard. 'That sounds fucking insolent to me.'

'Gentlemen.' Maynon's voice acid, 'I'd like to make the point that arms will probably be used in this raid. Chief Inspector Patchin, I think you'll agree that the Squad has a higher percentage of grade marksmen.'

'And if the Squad cocks it up?' Patchin queried. 'Then everyone will want to know why the Sweeney was dabbling in IRA affairs on a case that was already established as a Bomb Squad case.'

Ewing tapped Regan on the shoulder. 'What's happening?' he asked in a low voice.

'There are other people interested in the IRA. Everybody and his mother is looking for promotion.'

Ewing didn't understand. He was studying the back of Patchin's head which was wagging to emphasize the points he was making. And he was talking about Mavor and Declan Murray and Martha Williams, and it *did* sound as if it was Patchin's case all along and somehow the Flying Squad had stumbled on to it.

'What exactly is he trying to do?' Ewing making no attempt to keep his voice low.

'Patchin wants the raid and the Big Arrest,' Regan replied.

'You mean we could get the squeeze. We might not be there?'

'It's possible. Patchin has to be talked out of it—that's Maynon's job—otherwise he may go over Maynon's head.'

'Look, there's no time to fuck about,' Ewing said firmly.

Regan turned his back on Ewing and studied Maynon standing behind his desk, listening to the Patchin monologue, hiding so well his impatience. Eyes flickering for one second across the faces, and meeting Regan's.

Regan cut straight across Patchin summing up some argument. 'My opinion, sir, is that it has to be simple, small, competent numbers. It sounds as if Mr Patchin is trying to organize a charabanc party—'

'Shut your bloody mouth, Regan!' Patchin snapped.

'I have to interrupt you twice, Mr Patchin, sir. Our American friend here has pointed out there is a slight element of urgency—'

'What d'you mean American friend? What does that mean?'

Regan turned round automatically in Ewing's direction. Ewing had gone.

Haskins stepped in. 'What makes this a Bomb Squad case? It's a Gloucester CID Murder Squad case relating to the Mavor murder. The Flying Squad are also involved because Mavor was once a career informer of ours. I fail to see any connection with the Bomb Squad until we physically discover a bunch of IRA micks in the raid area.'

That started Patchin up again, and louder. Regan looked at his watch. He couldn't walk out of this meeting like Ewing, because his voice was needed. The meeting was critical. If everything went well on the farm then it didn't matter, but if there was a foul up, and normal practice was to plan for the possibility of things going wrong, then there would be an enquiry afterwards. The key question at any enquiry would be how was the raid set up, who were the command group, and why?

Regan was worried. Patchin was really digging his heels in. Declan Murray might die of old age before this argument was resolved. It was going to take time to resolve. Regan could see there was now a distinct possibility that he, Ewing, and the Flying Squad were going to lose the case to Patchin.

Len settled the Rover 3500 down to just under a hundred and ten.

As the Squad car shot past the airport spur on the M4, and into the Thames Valley constabulary, a white traffic Landrover with two astonished uniformed coppers pulled out and gave chase and got within about a half mile of them. Then Len gave three blasts on the Winkworth gong, and the Landrover dropped behind and disappeared. Only the Flying Squad had Winkworth gongs fitted to their Q-cars. Regan could imagine the gist of the conversation of the two in the white Landrover. 'Fucking Sweeney, who do they think they are?'

London to Bath took one hour fourteen minutes. Then they were turning right off the Lower Bristol Road and heading up past Royal Crescent, and then left along Weston Road and on to the B4421 towards Bristol. A mile along that Len made a right-hander.

ISLADE ½ MILE. Len indicated the signpost almost obscured by a small tree. He slowed the Rover down now, in the mud lanes. He didn't want to drive straight into Islade Farm. There was DCI Minshaw of Bath CID to find, the whole setup to be discussed with him, and his local knowledge absorbed. Like all busts, the important plan is not the assault on a house, farmhouse, whatever, it's the contingency plan if it goes amiss—when a house is rushed in order to grab a killer with a shotgun, and it's discovered too late that he's got hold of six schoolchildren as hostages.

They found an empty Austin Allegro parked by the side of

the road, one indicator, the nearside one, flashing. It was a standard issue station car, presumably Minshaw's—the indicator blinking to draw the attention of the approaching party from London.

Regan signalled to Len to pull over, and got out of the car fast. He headed up the fifty-yard incline towards the point where the road disappeared over a small hill. There was a line of bushes and trees crowning the hill. A man came through the trees. He had the cut of a plainclothes country copper: Harris tweed jacket, Viyella shirt, dark tweed tie, olive green trousers, but regular police issue black shoes. 'Who are you?'

'Detective Inspector Regan—Flying Squad.'

'Chief Inspector Minshaw.' He extended a hand for a perfunctory shake, then swung the hand to indicate the area left of the road beyond the hill. 'The farmhouse, just over the top—about twenty yards. I've seen two men.'

'Could there be others?'

'Could be fifty. It's a big place, perhaps fifteen rooms.'

'Description of the men, sir?'

Minshaw described them. One could've been Declan Murray. Maybe. Maybe not. Neither was Purcell. 'Tell me how you city gents think you're going to handle this?'

Regan told him how the London lot would be organized. He didn't tell him about the two-hour meeting in Maynon's office which had ended in an all-out row and Maynon pulling rank on Patchin. Patchin had gone off and tried to locate by phone one of his own superintendents, and had failed to do so. He had then no alternative but to accept Maynon's orders: Patchin and his members of the Bomb Squad to go to Bath CID and wait it out there; Regan, Carter, another DS from Regan's squad, Hille, and another complete squad under Inspector Cawder—ten men—to go to the

118

farm, armed. Also two uniformed sharpshooters. Also Superintendent Maynon. Eight cars, all to make their own way to Bath, or to the farm as quickly as possible.

Len and Regan knew they had a head start of ten minutes at least. Regan had signed out a Smith and Wesson .38 before the meeting, anticipating events. All the other coppers there had to find the armourer, fill in and sign forms, before setting off on the journey.

Minshaw and Regan moved carefully through the trees and along a windbreak to a point which Minshaw thought gave the best view down over the farmhouse. He pulled out an ancient pair of Leitz folding opera glasses, unfolded them, and handed them to Regan.

Regan panned the glasses down and across the large farmhouse in the hollow below. It was a Jacobean house, with some remnants of early Tudor. Typical stockbroker's weekend retreat. At the same time it was obviously a functioning farmhouse—tractor, geese, hay silo, cattle shed, automatic cattle-feedstuff troughs, and to the right of the house a high mound of polythene bags of nitrate fertilizer covered by a tarpaulin. A couple of horses in a paddock, and a small herd of cattle eating in the fields beyond. They were clustered in a close group for protection from the wind. A weak sun wandered around above the haze of low clouds, but the day was cold and the breeze fresh and cutting.

Regan took it all in at a glance. Not the finer points of the architecture of a house in an ideal setting amidst a hollow between two hills, but the tactical situation, the dead ground, and the ground cover.

There were features about the house which were distinctly bad news. A series of Bath stone walls enclosing small sheds and the paddock ran from the back of the house out and up to the tree windbreak that circled round to where they stood.

Several men would have to be deployed to the rear, maybe four. The Flying Squad had by their own insistence just a dozen or so men. For a second he wished he had the bull-necked Patchin from Bomb Squad and some of his six-foot oafs.

'I don't see anybody.'

'Main room left of front door, there was a bloke. Another man opened curtains in the bedroom three windows along the first floor, right of front door.'

Regan looked, studied first all the windows of the three floors of the farmhouse. He shook his head. No one in sight.

'There's a side exit to the house, the other side.'

Regan swung the opera glasses to the far end of the house.

'You won't be able to see it.'

'That cow-byre wall runs from front to rear down that side of the house?'

Minshaw nodded.

Regan turned at the sound of footfalls. Len came up. 'Mr Maynon's arrived, guv.'

'Who with?'

'Hille, and two sharpshooters, Derrecks and Porter.'

A moment later, Maynon, Sergeant Hille, and the two other uniformed sharpshooter sergeants carrying Remington rifles arrived under the trees. Maynon took the opera glasses, nodded to Minshaw. 'Long time no see, John. We'll have a beer and nostalgia if we survive this lot.'

'Two men in there.' Regan addressed the sharpshooters. 'The rear of the house looks to be the problem.'

'Armed, guv?' The sharpshooter introduced as Derrecks asked.

'There are no IRA Provos who aren't armed. Take the back. The rest of us will cover the front with small arms.'

Another two cars had arrived from London. Regan made his way back to the line of four cars, waving the plainclothes men to move the cars and conceal themselves off the road. They were DS's and DC's of his squad and Inspector Cawder's squad. He heard Maynon's voice floating back, a generalization Maynon was making to Minshaw, Len and others who had moved up the hill. 'An important thing to remember about this operation is that if it's a cock-up it's my balls cut off. . . .'

Maynon now signalling one car to take the risk. Four of Cawder's squad getting into it, the Smith and Wessons bulging the sides of their macs. The car heading off up and over the hill, into the hollow and beyond and up again over the crest of the next hill, to position itself on the west approach to the house.

A couple of traffic motorcyclists arriving up the lane, dispatched from Bath CID, to close the road. Maynon and Regan turning round at the noisy approach, both faces furious. That's how a balls-up begins—two coppers on motorbikes whose engine noise would waken the dead, blundering into the midst of the enemy camp.

A young sergeant now arriving out of a fifth car carrying the loudhailer—a new young bloke in Cawder's squad. Maynon signalling him and giving him the opera glasses and pointing to the low, dressed stone wall bordering the lane in front of the house, where he should take up his position. Maynon telling him what to say in the loudspeaker.

Regan moved through the trees and found a position where he could squat down and survey the entire front façade of the house. No sign of movement in the house. Some inevitable sounds of the operation around it. The crack of a twig breaking, a disturbed crow screaming out insolence and rising up through the trees. The sixteen men and the two motorcycle policemen more visible, disposing themselves in a wide circle round the building and outhouses.

Then Regan heard the sound of the Smith and Wessons being opened, and chambers checked.

Carter arrived. He had grabbed the sixth car from New Scotland Yard. He hadn't been ready when Regan was—he hadn't checked out a gun from the armoury. He answered Regan's unspoken question about why he should be last to arrive. 'Thought I'd check on where Lieutenant Ewing went when he disappeared from the meeting. Phoned his hotel. Did you know, guv, he checked out yesterday—gave no forwarding address?'

Regan didn't know. He started to think about Ewing and Tanya's little bed, and other thoughts about the American lieutenant.

The young sergeant with the loudhailer was now in position behind the wall and looking up in Maynon's direction. Maynon was standing, Smith and Wesson held low, in a clump of bushes five yards away from Regan. Maynon signalled with a wave of the gun.

The young sergeant switched on the loudhailer and the amplified voice hit the front of the farmhouse and reverberated up the hollow. 'You people in the house. This is the police. We are armed. You will all come out with your hands high in the air. I repeat, we are armed. You have two minutes. Then we will come and take you out.'

Silence. The little background song of birds terminated, the creatures shocked into silence by the loudhailer. All eyes on the house. No movement. Regan turned to look at Minshaw, the Bath CID guy who had seen two people, wondering if Minshaw was going to announce now that he might have been mistaken.

122

The young sergeant two hundred yards away studied his watch as if it would be his decision after two minutes to signal the armed police forward. Maynon signed for him to repeat the message.

The loudhailer clicked on again. 'You in there. This is the police. We're armed. Come out with your hands high in the air. Or we will use our arms. Come out now.'

Silence from the house. Not even the sound of the window that had banged in the wind twice in the last five minutes. No wind now.

Maynon's face a mask. He must make a decision, he and he alone. Another minute passed. He signalled the loudhailer sergeant to try a third announcement.

The loudhailer sergeant, half crouched behind the wall, brought his head up slightly, wondering if Maynon was signalling him to say the message again or abandon the loudhailer approach and join the others—it certainly looked as if the house was empty.

The young sergeant raised his head slightly, up from his crouch, so it was above the wall. Maynon screamed 'Down' at exactly the same second that Regan shouted 'Gun!' But the young sergeant didn't hear either of them. And anyhow he wouldn't have been able to separate the two commands bawled simultaneously at him. The young sergeant was dying. He was walking up the lane towards them, the loudhailer still gripped tight in his left hand, and his eyes still open, but just about to be flooded with blood from two round holes above them which looked like a second pair of eyes.

And the expression on the young sergeant's face was astonishment because he knew he was dead. And first he dropped the loudhailer, which rolled around crackling static, and then he fell himself. And no death throes. He fell and he was completely still.

Maynon's head switchbacked round, from Minshaw, who was nearest him, to Regan, who had been on his left. But Regan was already running along the tree line past Maynon and towards the lane. Minshaw had seen the wisp of smoke and maybe a sight of the gun. 'Carbine, room just above front door, slightly left.' Maynon put up his head. One of the police marksmen was crashing through the trees. He'd seen a colleague die. The shot had come from the front of the house. He and his fellow sharpshooter had been placed in a defensive or withdrawal position at the rear—and he wasn't having that. He disappeared again into the trees.

Maynon shouted at Minshaw, 'Get the loudhailer.' Minshaw, a man in his forties, was off and sprinting, using the tree-cover to get to the lane, and using the wall which lined each side of the lane to approach the dead sergeant and the loudhailer.

But already he'd interpreted Maynon's fear and knew it was too late.

The four police who had driven past the house were moving in unseen, except for the cordite contrails of their shots out of the bushes that ringed the perimeter of the farmhouse grounds.

'Stop firing!' Maynon shouted.

The police disobeyed. And they did it for two reasons. Because they were going to kill the copper-killer inside the farm, no trials, no fifteen-year murder sentences commuted for good behaviour. They were also going to disobey because Maynon would then be able to say at the enquiry that was bound to come that they, his men, had disobeyed him. And that would help to let Maynon off the hook for the balls-up of a dead copper. And Maynon's men liked Maynon and wanted him off the hook.

It was Regan who got to the loudhailer. 'Stop firing! Everybody stop firing!'

A string of shots greeted his order. But they were no longer fired by police. They came from the three marksmen inside the house.

'All police cease fire!' Regan sitting propped up behind the wall, four police within his view, guns out, looking at him, wondering what he'd do now, or later, if they did ignore him. A colleague had been killed, revenge had to happen now, before the issues were muddied over by the bastard barristers of defence counsel and the soft judges of lousy justice.

Maynon approached, doubled up, Minshaw behind him. They joined Regan behind the wall.

'Three. Sound like M64 carbines,' Regan suggested.

'Maybe more than three,' Maynon said, studying the crumpled form of the dead young sergeant ten feet away, fighting back emotion for the moment, to keep a clear head.

'We can get into the house, sir. The building's large enough. Three men can't cover four exterior walls.'

Maynon's brows sharp knit together. He was thinking it out for himself.

Silence all around again, except for the barking of a dog a quarter of a mile away, as it responded to the noise of the shooting.

'I think it's three men. That house has four walls. So one wall's uncovered. I'm going to find it,' Regan said.

'You stay here,' Maynon ordered sharply. But Regan had already started along the ditch, making up the lane to approach the west side of the house.

He stopped in his tracks. It was the sound of one single shot and a scream as a bullet hit home. But it seemed to come from inside the house. The scream climbed high and then sank suddenly, as somebody died noisily. It was the antithesis of the way the young copper had died. Regan's eyes looked back to Maynon and the eyes of the other policemen nearest him. What the hell could it mean? Committing suicide? Or topping each other inside the house?

Above the front door, a floor to ceiling window—almost a french window, except that there was no balcony outside. The man who had just been shot crossed the room and crashed out through the glass of the long window, down in a heap on the front doorstep.

Regan was momentarily confused. All police eyes on the white curtains of the room from which the body had crashed down, as if looking for more bodies to follow. Instead a deep voice came from behind the curtains.

'This is Lieutenant Ewing. Don't shoot. I'm going to open the windows.'

Maynon was already on the loudhailer before Ewing had finished speaking. 'There's a policeman in the house. Don't fire!'

The tall windows on the first floor opened—a gesture that seemed even more theatrical because one window had no glass. Ewing stood there—a spare, contemplative figure, apparently unconcerned about the possibility of a nervous copper loosing off a shot. He held his Navy Colt .45 in his hands.

Regan remembered the dumdum bullets, and the quality of the dying man's scream.

'Two other guys,' Ewing shouted. 'I think they're in the room on the east side. Three rooms on that side. They're in the middle one.'

Everybody now moving around to take covert looks at the east side of the house from behind the hedgerow bordering

126

the lane. Next to the east wall, and about twenty feet away and parallel to it, the brick wall of an out-house—it looked like a cow-byre. There were no windows or openings in the long wall of the byre, so there was no easy way to manoeuvre into any position where a view into the centre room on the east side could be gained.

Maynon was already issuing orders. Regan decided to opt out of whatever plan the Super had and suddenly moved off fast, in a difficult half-circle round and in on the far side of the byre. Meanwhile he could hear Maynon on the loud-hailer. Police were to enter from the west side of the house and proceed with care—Lieutenant Ewing to stay where he was, which could only be guessed at because he'd disappeared.

What a complete fuck up—Regan's analysis could arrive at no other conclusion. One cop dead, one of three possible suspects dead. Any more lunacy and all that anybody would gain from the operation would be the Bath undertaker.

Regan reached the byre. For reasons that weren't immediately apparent it was disused and cleaned out. Maybe the farm owner was using it as a garage or storage place. He went to the windowless wall that faced the east wall of the house with the two men holed up in the middle room. He was looking for any crack in the wall or a hole between wall and roof truss where he could get a sight of the east façade. There was nothing. He studied the wall. The byre must have been built during the war when local government relaxed the restrictions on the exclusive use of heavy Bath stone for building and allowed ordinary brick. Regan reckoned it was a single cavity brick wall. He turned round. Ewing was standing there. Ewing and he had been on the same wave-length, working out the same idea.

'I had to kill that guy,' Ewing offered to Regan's unasked question. 'He walked into me.'

'So we have two. We have to get them alive.'

'Okay, Jack Regan, how do we bust this wall and get them?' Ewing went over to the wall and fingered it as if he was going to find the answer in the tactile feel of it.

'A car?'

'The trouble with that,' Ewing said softly, 'is we don't get a second chance.'

Regan was already striding for the door.

Once outside he had to take a circuitous route to avoid Maynon. There was no time for talk. Fortunately the two men inside the farmhouse started to loose off some shots, some bouncing off the byre wall and slicing out into the road. Regan saw two coppers taking full precautions, noses stuck in the mud of the lane.

He found Len. It took him thirty seconds to explain to Len he was about to write off the car, then three minutes to get it into position. Carter came running. Carter knew that something was up—some intuitive knowledge that an event was about to occur where those taking part might end up in the line of promotion—and when Carter smelled something like that he was a difficult person to dissuade. 'Fuck off,' Regan said. He had no time to explain or argue. Carter retreated. Regan piled into the car beside Len, and the Rover dipped its rear axle and took off fast, over the crest, past Maynon and his group tucked in cautiously behind the hedgerows, then on down the lane to an open gate on the left. Len turned the car through the opening and moved it across the stubble earth to the byre.

Ewing got in the back, added some precise words of instruction to Len, wound down the rear window, and took out the massive Colt. Regan opened his Smith and Wesson, checked the chambers and closed it.

The Flying Squad car was sitting just outside the door of

the byre. The double doors of the byre were open. Regan signalled Len. Len revved the engine up to four thousand, then, using clutch slip to take up the first seconds of acceleration, piloted the car, tyres skidding, into the byre, and smashed the car into the west wall.

The wall detonated into a thousand separate brick pieces and a cloud of dust as the car sliced through. Len lost the windscreen but managed to slew the car sideways and brake so that Regan and Ewing were both facing the middle room in the east wall. Ewing saw a man with a gun pointed at him and fired. The face of the man spattered into a sheet of blood and dropped from sight. Regan hurled himself from the car and ran flat out for the window that Ewing's shot had disintegrated. He took a risk now that he didn't want to take. But there was no time, and he must have one witness.

He stuck his head in the window, his hand holding the gun straight out in front of him. He saw the redheaded man, carbine in his hand, turn. But the carbine was held loose. And the redhaired man saw Regan and knew there was no hope. The redhaired man looked back and down at his dead companion, the blood-smashed face unrecognizable, and he was stunned. Perhaps not even aware that Regan was pointing a gun at him. Perhaps not even aware of Regan, as he stepped over the window-sill, across the broken glass, and prised the M64 carbine from the man's hand.

Regan turned to Ewing, who was studying the scene from the window. 'Christ, don't stand there! Tell Maynon to call them off! This is the moment we get shot by mistake!'

Ewing carefully withdrew his head.

'What's your name?' Regan asked the redhaired man.

The redhaired man turned his head and for the first time really looked at Regan. And Regan knew certain things from the look. First, that this was Declan Murray. Second, that he was not going to talk. And third, that the whole case now rested on making him talk.

Maynon chose the dining room of the farmhouse for the gathering. Patchin and his men came in from Bath Headquarters. Also some senior, unidentified, Bath and Wells CID personnel.

Maynon sat at the top of a fifteen-foot-long oak refectory table. Some sat in upright wooden chairs—there were about a dozen chairs. Others stood around fidgeting. Maynon said nothing until the stage had been cleared—the photographing of the dead policeman and the two suspects completed, and the bodies taken off by ambulance. Then he set the stage. Six men were placed on the approach road out front, another three covered the rear—all armed and ready to grab unexpected visitors.

Nobody seemed anxious to hustle events. It was now four o'clock in the afternoon—the policemen's faces resigned, as if they really didn't expect the meeting to get off the ground until six.

Regan studied Patchin. Patchin had said not one word since he'd arrived at the farmhouse. He must obviously be pleased that Declan Murray was now in custody, but also he'd be livid at Maynon for losing the two others. He would be on about that for the rest of his life—that if he'd been in charge, he would've got all three alive. Patchin's silence was also the reaction to a dead copper—one that Patchin knew as vaguely as did Regan—and the copper had been in Regan's Flying Squad lot. But witnessing or being in the proximity of the death of a policeman on duty—the identification—had a brutalizing effect on the emotions. Patchin was also quiet because he was thinking, like everybody else

130

assembled there, about revenge—that two suspect police-killers were dead, but there was one who could still be punished.

Declan Murray had been placed inside a police car parked out of sight inside the byre. Sergeant Carter and another sergeant from Cawder's lot, guarding him. Carter, who was armed with a Smith and Wesson, was also given a Remington.

Regan studied the rear of the squat head. Patchin was sitting on a wooden chair midway between himself and Maynon, facing Maynon, back to Regan. Regan summed it up: the danger area in this room at this meeting was Patchin but, curiously, events had got so out of hand that Patchin might not give trouble. All right, raise objections that would be recorded in the minutes that would be written by a DI from Cawder's section. But give no trouble here in the farmhouse, because he was going to flay Maynon alive at the official enquiry which would happen within days.

'I don't want to spend a lot of time in useless talk. We have to clean up and clear off these premises as fast as possible. I wanted you all here to see this house—to see the difficulties we had assaulting it, and grabbing Murray. There will doubtless be an enquiry and some of you will be witnesses.' Maynon turned and addressed Patchin. 'I've just made a number of phone calls. One to your superior, Superintendent Mirren. He's agreed that Murray is possibly the most important find ever—and it does look as if this farmhouse is some kind of centre—and that others of the IRA Provos may turn up here.'

Patchin studied his police notebook, didn't look up at Maynon, made a couple of notes with a Bic.

'I've also obtained the co-operation of the Bath and Wells

Constabulary to take the unusual course of helping us to stage a fake accident on the M4. They will then issue reports that three men, one identified by driving licence as Declan Murray, have been killed in this accident.'

'What's that about?' Patchin asked, and paused, and added: '. . . sir?'

'It means, Mr Patchin, that we in the Flying Squad have evidence that Declan Murray and associates planned an important robbery, probably in London, using a group of people the rest of whom we would like to get into custody. If they learn that Murray's in police custody, they may take to their heels and we may never see 'em again. If they think he was killed in a car crash, they may remain in England long enough for us to interrogate Murray. And the information we get from Murray may secure their arrests.'

'A fake car crash? A little elaborate when the chances of getting information out of Murray are slim. Correct? Well, that's what I think.'

'It's what your superior officer thinks that matters, Mr Patchin,' Maynon said quietly. 'He agrees with me. There's a large job being drafted somewhere. We want our hands on the potential robbers. It's possible that they won't disappear in a puff of smoke if they see in the papers a photo of a wrecked car, and are convinced that their three compatriots lost their lives in a simple accident.'

'I understood that the first time you explained it, Superintendent,' Patchin said gently, obviously anticipating now that the enquiry into the Islade Farm deaths, whenever it happened, would find against Maynon. That meant any charges of insolence or insubordination that Maynon wanted to bring, say against Patchin, would be dismissed. Patchin pressed on. 'What makes you think, Superintendent, that you can hide the news of the death of your detective sergeant for days, weeks, perhaps months? What about his parents for instance? Or the press?'

'The operation of the IRA Provos is classified as a matter of national security and a D-notice will cover this affair and silence the press. I think I've had enough questions from you, Mr Patchin, especially as some of these answers are self-evident to us in the Flying Squad. If we tell the parents of Detective Sergeant Ross that in order to get the criminal associates of his murderers they must keep his death quiet for a while, they will do so. Our men in the Flying Squad are of the highest calibre—we tend to find that their parents reflect these qualities.'

Regan was struck by the irrelevance and emptiness of it all. Maynon and Patchin were now making speeches really for the sergeant who was taking the minutes of the meeting —quotes for the coming enquiry. Regan looked around. He'd been aware that Ewing had been present for the first minutes of the meeting, but then, guessing that it was descending into recriminations and backbiting, had quietly stepped out. Regan now followed suit.

He came out of the front door of the farmhouse and headed for the byre. He couldn't see the eight coppers who were probably watching him as he strode towards the byre. They, and colleagues to relieve them, would be stuck out there under bush and tree cover for weeks, perhaps, waiting to grab others of the gang or anybody who so much as turned a car off the road and into the drive of the farmhouse.

Something was wrong. Regan quickened his pace to a run. He could see Len to the left of the byre tinkering inside the raised bonnet of the wrecked Rover. He could see the hole in the byre wall. But he could see no car, no

Carter, no Declan Murray in the byre. Just the other detective sergeant sitting on a heap of rubble having a covert smoke.

Regan ran in through the gap in the byre wall. 'Where are they?' he shouted.

The young sergeant jackknifed to his feet. 'Who, sir?'

'The prisoner Murray, and Sergeant Carter—who the fuck else?'

The young sergeant instantly realized that something was wrong. 'The American came. . . .'

'Lieutenant Ewing?'

'I think Sergeant Carter called him Ewing. He said Mr Maynon's orders were to proceed to London. They went off—'

'Ewing, Carter, the suspect Murray—the three went off in the car?'

'Right, sir.'

Regan's heart sank. He saw with appalling clarity that Ewing had to steal Murray, and that he, Regan, should have realized this. And he knew exactly what Ewing intended to do with Murray.

Regan sat alone in his office at one end of Squad Office, Maynon alone in his office at the other end, near the Reserve Room. They hadn't talked since Islade Farm. Haskins had gone off somewhere. Everybody else kept clear. Phone-callers were told to call back later. It was ten-fifteen. Neither Regan nor Maynon had eaten. Len had wordlessly brought Regan a coffee. No one had dared go near Maynon. Ewing or Carter would either phone or just walk in. Nothing to be done until that happened. Regan sat looking out of the window into the black and rain of the London night, mind racing, chain-smoking, going over all the facets of the

134

cock-up this afternoon. The unnecessary deaths, the inde-
cision, no person to blame but Maynon to shoulder all
responsibility. But actually they'd want more heads than
just Maynon's. Perhaps some votes for Regan. And that
wonderful finale, the unthinkable finale—two lunatics out
there with Declan Murray. Sergeant Carter, ludicrously
ambitious, deciding in his omnipotence that, yes, he would
be the Sweeney representative on the scene when Murray
divulged all. But what a risk to take. When you kick somebody around, occasionally they die. Or the other possibility: Declan Murray might well turn the tables on both
of them.

Regan could well visualize how it had happened. The
tall American walking into the byre, taking Carter aside
and putting it to him. What were the chances of getting
Murray to talk under the soft soap, Geneva Convention,
jokey, white as the driven snow, British Police interrogation
methods? None. At the same time, Murray had to talk. At
the same time, there were methods whereby Murray might
respond to questioning. Results could be got, whereby a
man like Ewing, who was after all just a tourist, could
wring the appropriate confession out of Murray. From no
co-operation to a flood of words. And Carter would just
simply have to be present, and take it all down. But out
of that it might suddenly become Carter's case, and no
longer Regan's.

Regan shouted to one of his sergeants, Walmesly, on the
other side of the partition wall: 'Terry. Anything in the
hospitality cupboard?'

Walmesly entered the office carrying a bunch of keys.
The keys were usually with the Duty Officer, who this week
was Haskins. Haskins—a rare chink of humanity in an
otherwise impervious exterior—always gave the hospitality

135

cupboard keys to Regan's sergeant. The sergeant opened the cupboard and displayed the remnants of three bottles of scotch, one of gin, and a very large bottle full of something.

'What's that great thing?'

The sergeant studied it. 'Half imperial gallon of Old Grandad the FBI sent for our half-hour's work on the Siranem case.'

'I'll have a small scotch.' Regan did partake of Old Grandad on occasions—it was just that he felt cool about any form of American police institution at the moment.

By midnight Regan was worried. He wondered what Maynon's state was. At eleven, Sergeant Walmesly had come back into Regan's office, given Regan a wink and a nod back towards Maynon's part of the world, and opened the hospitality cupboard again. He took out a half-bottle of gin and three bottles of tonic.

At twenty minutes past midnight Maynon walked in.

Regan looked up at his ice cold eyes. 'Any news?'

'Ewing just dropped in to my office for a few minutes.'

Regan made to get up. 'Where is he?'

'Gone. He left a typed report.'

'A report?'

'Declan Murray's coughed up. Everything. He's talked about Purcell. Names and all details of a planned bank raid. The lot.'

'Where's Murray?'

'Why?'

'Where's Declan Murray?' Regan's voice sharp and hard.

Maynon shrugged off his responsibility. 'Middlesex Hospital.'

'Why the fuck is he in hospital?'

'I don't know anything about it.'

'Where's this report?'

'You won't be reading it. Haskins put you on the case when it was concerned solely with the death of an ex-snout of yours. Now it's something different. I'm taking you off the case.'

Regan's face couldn't conceal his contempt.

'Detective Sergeant Carter will now . . .' Maynon started to say. But Regan was already heading for the door.

'Jack Regan!' The sharpness of Maynon's voice stopped him. 'You always justified the way you blustered and bullied your way round Squad Office by saying you got results. Well, you haven't done it in this case. Carter has.'

Regan walked out and slammed the door hard enough for fifty detectives around Squad Office to wonder for a few seconds if a small bomb had gone off. Then they decided it hadn't, and resumed their work.

'Right arm fractured, two places. Jaw fractured, two places. The fingers of one hand crushed. Index fingers and thumb broken. Lacerations and bruising on face. His head injuries are serious, actually—he's badly concussed. He's in shock.' The young Registrar of the Middlesex Hospital studied Regan sceptically. 'The Detective Sergeant "Castle" or something . . .' He'd forgotten the name.

'Carter.'

'Carter, yes the one who brought him in said the man Declan Murray had been in a car accident. . . .' He looked at Regan for his confirmation. Regan said nothing.

The young doctor's eyes went down to the Accident Department's Diagnostic Card on the desk in front of him. 'I've seen the victims of a hundred car accidents, Inspector. They're our stock in trade. This man's injuries weren't caused by a car accident.'

'I have to speak to him urgently.' Regan looked at his watch as if minutes counted. In fact he'd lost track of time. It was one-thirty in the morning.

'The earliest you'll speak to him is tomorrow midday. Another thing,' the young doctor was playing it cool, 'if this unfortunate man Murray was in a car accident, why is it that PC Ridge Taylor, one of our local bobbies, is sitting in the men's ward with a revolver lying in his lap?' Then he dropped his voice in a conspiratorial manner, 'May I ask you a private question?' He paused for effect. 'What's this fucking country coming to?'

Too many scenes like this, thought Regan. I've been in too many hospitals taking too much stick from too many young doctors for too long. And many of them right, like this bloke tonight. But that wasn't the point. I'm getting old, thought Regan, that's the point. And tonight they are trying to write me off, and substitute the name 'Carter'. Well, not yet—he'd be giving them and Carter a few more headaches before they wrote him off.

He timed his return to the Yard for three am dead on. He told Len to go home, and that he'd get a cab. Len drove off.

Regan showed his ident to the two security sergeants on the doors, and took one of them aside. 'Maynon, DCI Haskins—gone?'

'The Chief Inspector went at midnight. Superintendent Maynon about five minutes ago.'

Regan headed for the row of lifts.

Detective Chief Inspector George Heller had his feet up on his desk and was practising the art of putative sleep, real sleep that could be snapped out of in a second if something went wrong. Heller was a DCI of forty-three, two years off retirement, tough, and trusted by everyone. Regan gave a perfunctory knock on the door. Heller's eyes came open wearily.

'Guv, did the Day Duty Officer, Chief Inspector Haskins, give you the keys when he went off?'

'Why, Jack?'

Regan could see the bunch of keys on the desk in front of Heller.

'Did he mention I could have a shufti at some "scene of crime" photos from the safe in his room?'

'No.'

'Funny,' Regan acted surprised. 'Anyhow I need the keys to his safe.'

'Grab,' Heller said, sitting back in his chair rearranging his feet on the desk-top.

Regan turned to the door.

'Jack, you're lying to me.' Heller's cool eyes fixed on him unwavering for a moment. Then the left eye produced a wink. 'You want those keys to poke about a bit. You don't have to lie to me, Jack. I root for you against Carter or any other of those young shits. I'm on your side, Jack, 'cos in the final analysis you're a harder bastard than this whole shower put together. That I hand you as a fact.'

Regan nodded slowly. 'Thank you, guv,' he said, and walked out.

Heller closed his eyes and was asleep.

He found it, not in Haskins', but in Maynon's safe. Pinned to the top of the report was a note to Maynon's secretary. 'Xerox one copy, forward to Head of Bomb Squad by nine am latest.'

Regan lifted the note. The front page of the five-page report was entitled: 'Reference planned bank raid, New

York Bank and Trust Campany, 300 Eastcheap, London EC3. Source Declan Murray. Report by Detective Sergeant Carter, Flying Squad.'

Two things struck Regan immediately. First that Ewing was letting Carter take all the credit—no mention of Ewing's name on the title page. The second was the type-face of the typewriter that had been used for the report. The n's and the l's were bent. Whenever she had typed a report for him, and it had happened many times, often in the small hours of the morning, he had promised her that one day he would buy her a new typewriter. He wondered if Ewing, seeing the bent type-faces of the report he'd dictated, had made Tanya the same promise.

Sɪᴛᴇx ᴘʀᴏᴊᴇᴄᴛᴇᴅ ʟᴏɴᴅᴏɴ ʙᴀɴᴋ ʀᴀɪᴅ ʙʏ ᴍᴇᴍʙᴇʀs ᴏf ᴛʜᴇ ᴘʀᴏᴠɪsɪᴏɴᴀʟ ɪʀᴀ

From: Detective Sergeant Carter.

Distribution: DCS Maynon, DCI Haskins, only.

Source of information: James Declan Murray.

sᴜʙᴊᴇᴄᴛ: Manner of robbery of the New York Bank and Trust Company, 300 Eastcheap, London EC3 by group (listed). Projected date of robbery: approximately forty-eight hours from this date time (qualified). Action required: immediate.

Report commences.

The Provisional IRA group listed:

1 Thomas Edward Murphy, 27, address unknown.

2 James Kavanagh, 50, address unknown. Nicknamed 'The Broker.'

3 Edward James Traynor, believed to be early 20s, address unknown.

4 Tom George Martin, nationality Scots. Connections with SNP (Scottish Nationalist Party), last address (parents) 14 Royal Street, Greenock; not seen six months. Considerable record including Larceny Dwelling House and Armed Robbery, CRO no 6770/69.

5 Harold James Evans, nationality believed Welsh. Cross ref possible connect with Harold T. Evans, Welsh Nationalist, CRO no 8101/71. Record GBH and Assault with Deadly Weapon. CRO no 6240/69.

141

6   Thomas Edward Parrish, early 20s, address unknown.

7   Howell Joseph McEvoy, early 20s, address 216 Queen Anne's Terrace, Liverpool.

8   Joe John Everitt, believed 25, address Orneskill Street, Belfast. Record of minor crime.

9   Terence Feeney, regular officer Irish Army gone Absent Without Leave October 1971. Address unknown. Suspect safe blown on two bank robberies in Republic of Ireland. Member of right-wing Irish Republican groups.

10   Patrick (Pascal?) Timothy Harrington, 104 Queen's Crescent, Belfast. Age over 40. Convicted bank robber, CRO no 3195/62.

11   James Purcell, alias Eddie Christopher, alias Hunt Kalman, US citizen, details on file. Draftsman.

12   Cathy or Katey Traynor. Little is known about this girl. No relation to Edward James Traynor (see 3). Believed to be in early 20s, graduate Sociology, University College, Dublin; description fits girl suspect wanted in connection with bomb outrages Birmingham late 1971.

13 & 14   John Murphy and Joey O'Horgan, shot to death, Islade Farm, near Bath.

15 & 16   Brothers Tim and Tony Noonan, 18 Observatory Garden, Belfast City. No convictions. These two men suspect for three bank raids in the Republic. Reference Dublin Special Branch, telephone 0102 933120. *Note:* This writer has been in touch with Dublin Special Branch. They believe they have photos of half of suspects listed above. They will proceed wirephoto urgently.

INTENTION: The above group intend to rob the New York Bank and Trust Company within forty-eight hours. The writer of this report has been in contact with a police source who has knowledge of the type of operation of this kind of American bank in London and believes that this bank may carry large quantities in cash and convertible bonds. The writer of this report did not wish to jeopardize the security of the investigation by contacting any employee of the bank.

METHOD:

A   The New York Bank and Trust Company has two branches in London. 300 Eastcheap and 221 Curzon Street. The Eastcheap branch is the largest. Vice President: Averill Harben.

B   The New York Bank and Trust Company shares a security system with twelve other American banks in London including Interbank of Chicago, and Anglo-American Equity Bank Company. The security consists of a direct electronic link from all these banks to a central security office in South Audley Street. In the event of a break-in occurring in one of these banks, sensing apparatus sends a silent signal to the security office at South Audley Street. Two security guards leave the office and go to the appropriate branch to investigate. In the event of the security alarm having been set off by accident, these guards will investigate the bank premises before summoning the local police.

C   Purcell's plan is:

(1)   To deliberately set off the electronic alarm system in the New York Bank and Trust Company at Eastcheap.

(2)   To have others of his group abduct the two security guards as they step from the office in South Audley Street. Purcell believes the group will not expect to walk straight into their guns.

(3)   To relieve the guards at gunpoint of the keys to the Eastcheap bank.

(4)   To proceed with the guards and rendezvous with the rest of the group at the bank.

(5)   To gain entrance to the bank using the security guards' keys.

(6)   The gang will then change into police uniforms which they will have brought with them.

(7)   They will then use thermic lance equipment to cut open the safe and remove as much of the contents as possible and load a lorry at the back of the bank.

(8)   In the event of other police or civilians arriving, they trust that the sight of uniformed police already investigating inside the bank will allay suspicion. Four men will be exclusively involved in loading the lorry at the rear of the premises, the others in posing as policemen.

(9)   They time the raid as taking twenty-eight minutes from entering the bank to leaving in the lorry.

(10)   They will all be armed and are dangerous.

(11)   Purcell has been told that prior to the raid he will be taken to a secret address and kept under observation. After the raid they will hand over his share and release him. He has said that he is prepared to accompany them on the raid. They are considering his offer.

CONCLUSION: The information is the result of a lengthy interview with suspect Declan Murray. His attitude was one of co-operation throughout. We have no reason to doubt that he was telling the truth. This report has been written speedily for obvious reasons. The below signed will be pleased to discuss and clarify any points that may require amplification.

Signed: G. Carter
Detective Sergeant,
Flying Squad. C.O.C.8.

L ieutenant Ewing woke and adjusted his eyes to the darkness of the bedroom, and then raised and turned his head slowly to see the digital clock on her side of the bed. Four-thirty am. The beginnings of grey dawn seeping in at the edge of the chintz curtains. He raised himself on his elbow. Her hand came out and touched his. He told her softly to go back to sleep. He swung his legs over the side of the bed and explored the immediate area of carpet with his toes. They had made love a few hours ago, two hours of it. It had been good. He felt relaxed. It was all working out. The case was sewed up—except for his play—when he turned his cards face up, and watched the shock strike across all their faces.

His toes found the beer cans and pushed them away. Tanya had gone from fury to mirth when he'd produced the six-pack of beer at the bedside. 'Are you saying you're going to screw me and drink beer at the same time?'

He was watching her, his face had a quizzical expression, his head inclined. 'What about it?'

'Are you mad? Are you crazy?'

'Thirsty,' he said.

'You are saying we are actually going to screw while you are drinking beer?' The anger was going and she was beginning to laugh.

He shrugged. 'Let's say screwing comes first—the beer is the intervals.' His eyes went slowly down the naked length of her body. 'But we start with an interval.' He

145

snapped off the beer can top one handed, and dropped it on the carpet by the bed. Over the next two hours five more tabs and six empty cans of beer ended up on the floor.

He got up and headed across the room. 'What's the time,' she asked, her voice soft and vague.

'Four-thirty. I'm making a States call, collect. I'll be back. Go sleep.'

'What happens if I don't want to sleep? What happens if I want a screw again?'

He paused at the door. 'We're out of beer.'

She sighed, pulled the sheets up and over her head. He went out of the room and pulled the door closed.

In the sitting room he picked up the scotch bottle on the way to the phone. He picked up the phone and dialled 108. He got through straight away.

'Which country are you calling?' a tired voice enquired.

'USA, San Francisco.'

He was connected to the States operator. 'I'd like to make a collect call to Parry, Duty Officer, Main Bay, San Francisco P.D., Area Code 415 444-0900, my name is Ewing.' He said it all in one sentence.

He unscrewed the whisky cap and took a small swig, and studied his watch. Four-thirty equals eight-thirty pm, coast time, a good moment to catch Parry coming on to night watch and just about to start on patrol.

It took the operator another ten minutes to get through and locate Lieutenant Parry, Ewing's closest colleague in Frisco P.D.

Parry came straight on the line with a question. 'How goes it?'

'Ed, it's working out. We're going to find him.' Ewing paused as if suddenly he wondered about whether there

146

was any real purpose in this phone call. The issues had always been laid out—why check back? The answer was he needed that final confirmation that they were backing him and he was not alone. 'Ed, I want to know nothing's changed. That I proceed with the plan that you and Dane and Darrel put up. I don't want to hear later that any of you guys had last minute thoughts.'

Lieutenant Parry was also silent for a moment, and then said two words of affirmative. Ewing was to proceed and execute the plan that they had all discussed and agreed to.

Sunday morning around nine o'clock. Regan walked up from the village into the tree-line. The paths which led through pines to the valley escarpments were empty except for a couple of goats which scattered from him and leapt off awkwardly to hide in the clumps of wild fern. The trees of the valley were being stirred by the first hints of another storm. The air was cold, tightening the skin on his face. He found an eyrie of broken rock and climbed up to a perch which looked down on the falling land.

A church bell banged a truncated sound somewhere in the isolation below. Over the tiny world of Gloucester villages other bells echoed, as if to make the point of being ignored. He sat down on the rocks, took out his binoculars, and studied the farmhouse a quarter of a mile below. Then he panned round the quarter of a mile radius with the farmhouse in the centre. He could see no other policemen in bushes, gullies, or behind trees, armed with guns and binoculars. But there were policeman out there, at least half a dozen of them. Perhaps a couple of them had already seen through their binoculars Regan arrive on the rock, and had wondered what the hell he was doing there.

Because the word was out that Detective Inspector Regan

wasn't on the case any more. The case had been carved up last night between the Commander of the Flying Squad and the Superintendent of the Bomb Squad. When Regan had phoned through at six am this morning to ask what was the result of the O-Group, Haskins had said: 'Make sure we have your telephone number for wherever you'll be today.' Which meant fuck off. Sergeant Carter, according to Haskins, was 'unavailable on a job', which meant that Carter, interrogator and report-writer *par excellence,* had now replaced his superior, Regan, in spearheading the case for the Squad.

The house was a smaller version of the Islade farmhouse. There were four cars and a van parked around the mud yard in front of the house. Declan Murray, under Carter and Ewing's interrogation, had come up with the news that the group had a 'double stop'. They'd rented two farmhouses within a mile of each other. If the security of one blew out, there would be the other.

Whoever was heading the group now—Declan Murray had suggested it would be James Kavanagh—had decided that Islade had blown out. Probably related to Declan Murray's and his two pals' 'fatal accident'—a photo of their tin-opened car smashed over the M4, with suitable caption, on the front page of the *Daily Express*: IRA SUSPECTS KILLED IN M4 CRASH. Kavanagh would be worried that perhaps on one of the three dead bodies would be the Islade Farm address. Bath CID, who had been watching Islade Farm, said no one had turned up after the farm battle yesterday.

Obviously the people wandering around in the farmyard below had no idea that yesterday there had been a gun battle at Islade. Obviously they believed the M4 crash story. Regan could see a half a dozen of them clearly, going in and out of the farmhouse, loading up the van, no apparent haste. He could see their expressions, read their silence, understand their grief at what they considered an idiot stroke of Fate—their leader and two compatriots killed in a car hours before the job. Regan questioned the thought again and again. There was no other conclusion to come to. If they suspected that the accident was a fake, they'd be running around down there like a bunch of Keystone Cops getting the hell out.

The cold chilled him. He took out the letter and buttoned his coat up to the collar. The letter had come in yesterday's second post. Last night he'd read it quickly, now he read it again.

> Dear Jack,
>
> I am leaving you. I don't understand you and now I don't want to. This has nothing to do with the American Ewing. Next week I go on business to Germany. If you wish to see me I will agree, although I believe when you have thought about this, you will understand that contact between us is now pointless. There was much that happened in our relationship that I'll always thank you for, and I will never forget you.
>
> Good-bye, Jack Regan,
> Tanya.

He felt a sudden stab at the thought of the loss of her, her companionship, her genuine humour, and her confidence in all situations. And he'd miss her at night, too. He had had some of the best hours of his life with her, but one of them was always a victim in the relationship— it didn't matter who—and the seeds of its collapse were built in because of his work and his attitude to his work,

149

the seriousness with which he took his work. And the catalyst for the breakdown had to come sooner or later. Now was a good time. He was tired of most things and puzzled by himself, and unsure why he had been driven to take certain critical directions over the last years which he knew intuitively were wrong. Why didn't he question more his way of life? He knew he was losing finesse in his work. He knew that the respect of his enemies, and his colleagues —and most of his colleagues were enemies in some disguise —was gradually being tempered by the odd doubt. Here he was, on a Sunday morning, perched on a rock above the village of Barton, alone, no sergeants with him, not officially in charge of anything—what the fuck was he doing here? A robbery was going to take place in London tonight or tomorrow. Probably an enormous operation had been mounted by Maynon and the Bomb Squad brigade and he, Regan, didn't know a damn thing about it, was not privy to one jot of information about the over-all plan. Why?

Better question: why put up with it?

Answer: he knew he was hanging around, hanging on to this case, because there was something wrong about the whole fucking set-up as delineated by smart-arse Sergeant Carter in his worthy report. Something wrong. Something in that list of names. Something about the bank, perhaps? But what? Regan put the binoculars to his eyes and panned them across the farmhouse again. Still those men slowly loading the van.

Then he saw the girl come out. What was her name— Cathy or Katey Traynor? She was carrying something that looked like a transistor radio. Early twenties, undistinguished face, good body, good tits under a little cotton shirt, good arse, tight in Levis. Walks well. Yes, he, Regan, could give her one, give her a couple as a matter of fact. But no

150

other member of the Metropolitan CID had those plans for her. This kid was walking, walking beautifully, into a lot of trouble.

It *was* a transistor radio. Probably they would use it on the job to tune into police VHF transmissions.

Regan wondered if he was the only one on this Sunday in this Christian country who realized that Carter's report was junk. There certainly was one person who'd know for sure. But he wouldn't have read it—the draftsman James Purcell. And that was a possible area that might be worth studying as a starting point. The proposition: the report is a turd because the micks wouldn't have brought in such a bleeding high-powered piece of machinery like Purcell to do something so straightforward as to knock a bank over. Or would they? Or would they?

He lit a cigarette, propped the binoculars on his nose with one hand, held the cigarette in the other, smoking, contemplating the creatures in the farm below.

He couldn't understand why, but for some reason he felt sorry for them. He had been in Canada one winter on a National Service training thing, and he was with some hunters who'd been shooting wolves for fun—practice for the real game they were after. The beasts were being picked off as they came into the circles of the camp fires, starving, driven crazy by the smell of food. And the hunters had shot at them monotonously through the night, and Regan had felt an odd compassion for the ugly creatures howling and dying in the snow. The IRA Provos group were animals. That was the official line at the Yard. Animals, killers. But to Regan, in one sense, they were genuine, and hopelessly courageous. For a moment he was almost moved to warn them, advise them, but he knew they had already gone too far in one direction where they couldn't be saved.

Their experience of crime and killing had hardened them to a point of no return, the point beyond trust. If he wandered down there now and chatted to them, told them that the police knew most of the details of the bank raid, they'd run for it, cancel that bank, and start to plan another robbery. They were self-defeated within the terms of the great political and humanitarian ideas that they wanted society to subscribe to. Nonetheless he felt a certain sadness, because suddenly, in the close-ups of the binoculars, they looked their ages, and some of them, like the girl, were young. They were just too bloody young and pitiable to be mixed up in this.

He watched them load the thermic lance steel-cutting equipment into the van. He made a mental note of the bits and pieces as they loaded. Thermic lances, rods, step-up transformer, hydrogen and oxygen cylinders, asbestos face masks, normal steel-bar cutting equipment, assorted boxes, probably containing electrical equipment for re-circuiting alarm systems. It was almost as if they were parading each item for the blag specifically for the benefit of his binoculars, and in order for him to check the equipment.

They set off about one. The van first, and then the three private cars. He swung his binoculars down the road and up to a leafy lane that would intersect the road. He saw a Morris Marina pull out and head down, three heavy-looking plainclothes policemen aboard. Not Sweeney faces—presumably Bomb Squad.

Then he saw another squad car appear down the lane to the right of the farmhouse. The two police cars tucked in together, and began to tail the IRA procession at a discreet distance. They were all heading east. That meant Bath, and the London Road.

Regan stood up. He could see movement at the back of

the farmhouse and then half a dozen coppers appeared out of thin air and headed in towards the farmhouse. Well, he didn't want to get mixed up in that. Nothing was going to come out of a search of the farm. Nothing but the necessary formality of police procedure.

Next stop Middlesex Hospital and Declan Murray, the man who perhaps had the key to his theory about Carter's report as a heap of crap—assuming that Declan Murray would talk, a ridiculous assumption. He wandered down the track, scattering pebbles, heading for his car.

Lieutenant Ewing sat in the office at 300 Eastcheap and studied the Vice President of the bank. His name was Averill Harben. He was a New Yorker, and like all New York businessmen had been difficult to nail for a quick appointment. The entire resources of Scotland Yard had been mobilized. It was now Sunday and twelve pm. It had taken a full twelve hours to locate the man. His wife knew he had gone to Brussels on Saturday. The Yard knew that no one of that name had taken a scheduled air flight on Saturday in that direction. Next, they located some other employees of the bank and impressed them of the seriousness of the situation. A man had told them the address of Harben's mistress. They found Harben and the mistress in her flat in Chelsea. Harben had then insisted on checking with Head Office New York by telex. The directive giving Harben permission to co-operate fully with Ewing of SFPD, and the Yard, had taken two more hours.

Midnight on Sunday in the deserted business area of the City of London, and Ewing watched Harben turn grey as he read Carter's report. It took four minutes. At the end of it the American bank Vice President said: 'I don't believe it.'

Ewing studied him and wondered about it. 'Would you show me the bank's main safe, sir?'

Harben led the way across the marble floors of the empty bank. There were a few blue lights giving just enough light to show the way. There was a short flight of steps ending in a basement foyer which was closed off at one end by a wall of horizontal chrome steel bars, with a steel bar door set into it. Two yards behind the steel wall lay the safe.

'You're one hundred per cent sure that no one resembling the photo of James Purcell, the FBI photo I showed you, ever came to see you or anyone else in this bank?'

'How can I speak for my personnel?' the Vice President demanded stiffly. 'I saw no one resembling the FBI photograph.'

'But Purcell could have seen somebody else in this bank?'

'I'm saying he could have.'

'Like who?'

'My Assistant Vice President, Mr. Kreinhof.'

'How do I locate him?'

'You don't.' Mr Harben glowered. 'He went off two days ago on his spring camping holiday in the Adirondacks, as he does every year at this time. And running around in a camper truck with his kids, he will not be locatable.'

Ewing shrugged that off, then pointed to the safe. 'Could I see inside it?'

'Impossible.'

'Why impossible?'

The Vice President studied Ewing with an expression that suggested the American cop was being deliberately stupid. The expression also suggested that he felt that Ewing was in some way responsible for this projected bank robbery and that certainly he must take part-blame for the appalling

154

intrusion of privacy, in Scotland Yard tracking down and revealing a Chelsea mistress. 'A security device prevents this safe from being opened before nine am tomorrow morning even though myself and others are in possession of its combination.' The Vice President's voice was cold. 'You say that IRA Provisionals have thermic lance equipment. There's no protection against thermic lance, but my guess is it would take at least ten hours to cut through, first, the steel-bar wall, and then into the safe itself.'

'That sounds like overstaying a weekend in your bank?'

'Yes.'

'In other words, if we left this bank now and these guys broke in, there's not enough time for them to cut open the safe before your staff arrive in the morning.'

'Correct.'

'So maybe some other time soon they get their thermic lance together and rob the safe. What do they find? How much money is in the till?'

'Obviously I've no idea of an up-to-the-minute accounting.'

'Roughly how much?'

Mr Harben sighed. He was a precise man and he didn't like rough calculations. 'Many thousands of pounds sterling cash, say one hundred thousand. About thirty thousand dollars cash. And we hold customers' stock certificates, mainly US, and convertible, to the tune of perhaps quarter of a million sterling.'

Ewing's head inclined slightly to one side as he studied the safe and thought about it. He also studied the clock over the safe that timed the mechanism to open the safe at nine am. He remembered he'd seen that clock more or less on every bank safe back home. 'That's a lot of money,' he said softly. He'd done a quick calculation—it had come out at approximately three hundred and seventy thousand pounds sterling, or a piece off a million US dollars even.

'So if you've seen what you've come to see perhaps you'd be so good as to let me have the names of the personnel at New Scotland Yard that you've been dealing with. So I can liaise our security company with them.'

Ewing gave the names and left the bank. It was twenty minutes past midnight. He found a cab and gave Tanya's address. He reached her flat at a quarter to one and gave a tentative ring on the bell, loud enough to get her attention if she was awake, not loud enough to disturb her if she was asleep—or so he hoped. There was no response. He had asked the cab to wait. He got back into it and headed for the hotel in Bayswater Road.

He went up to his bedroom, took off his clothes and had a shower, then lay naked on top of the bed.

He picked up the phone and called the Yard. He told Squad Office switchboard it was an emergency and they gave him Superintendent Maynon's home number. He dialed the Surbiton number. Ewing had worked out why Declan Murray had not lied as they broke him, but had told them the truth. Everything he had said was truthful; there was no denying that. He had told them the truth— exactly half of it. Jesus, why hadn't they gone on and questioned him further? Why had they accepted a list of people, and the address of a bank, and decided that was it?

'Maynon.' A gruff tired voice on the end of the line.

'Lieutenant Ewing, Mr Maynon. Apologies for the hour. Wondered if you would do something for me very urgently in connection with our case. Could you put me on to somebody who could tell me all about electricity in London—by which I mean phases, wattages, voltages, etcetera, etcetera?'

There was a pause. It had nothing to do with Maynon's surprise at the request. Stranger requests had been made to him before at even later hours. He was working it out. 'I think there is someone who could help. Chap called Edward Terry. Very good friend. Used to be in the Min of Supply during the war. Chief Administrator now, the UK Grid System. He'd know most of that or he could refer you. Can I ask you what this is about?'

Ewing took the phone away from his ear and looked at it and considered. He had come to England to do a job. He had needed the help of Scotland Yard. Now he didn't need their help any more. For what he was about to do he positively didn't want them around any more. 'Some other time,' he said. He put the phone down.

Midnight. Regan strode the corridors on the fourth floor of Scotland Yard, wondering what would happen if the entire clientele of the Hilton Hotel were murdered in their beds now, policemen being a bit thin on the ground—it had taken him two hours to find where a bloody photo was filed. He banged his foot on the steel scuff-plate, and elbowed open the double doors of C11, Criminal Intelligence Department. 'You Lawler?'

A young sergeant dropped *The Sporting Life* over the floor in the move to his feet. 'Yes, guv.'

'Sergeant Lawler, you have somewhere in this museum of junk,' he slapped his hand down on the top of one of fifty, four-drawer, steel filing cabinets, 'the details of a caper, ref 202/71, entitled "Westminster Bank, Letchworth", subtitled "Failure to Rob Same". And although I'm in a rush I'm going to give you all of five seconds to find it.'

It took Lawler twenty minutes.

157

Regan opened the bulky file and slopped the contents over the top of the desk. He was not interested in the Westminster Bank raid, Letchworth, ref 202/71, or in the fact that it had failed. He was interested in a photograph he had seen once upon a time of what the villians left behind. This particular bunch of idiots had not realized that a thermic lance made a lot of smoke in the process of cutting through steel, and that this smoke must be ducted away, out of the back of a building. In the case of the Westminster Bank raid, Letchworth, ref 202/71, the smoke from the thermic lance work in the vault had got up the stairs, into the bank proper. An old age pensioner walking his cat had seen what he thought was the bank on fire at six am Monday morning. Within minutes, four large thugs were fleeing from the nozzles of the Letchworth Fire Brigade.

They left all their equipment. The photo Regan had been searching for was the police photo of the complete thermic lance equipment lined up along the wall at the back of the bank. The Westminster Bank raid, Letchworth, ref 202/71, was in fact the first time that thermic lance equipment had been used by criminals to attempt to cut open a safe in England.

'Is there anything else I can do for you, guv?' Sergeant Lawler asked, a little peevish at the amount of activity he'd had to perform to find the file—it being well after midnight, and usually, in C11, that was *Sporting Life* time.

'Coffee,' Regan ordered, his eyes concentrating on the photograph, ticking off the items that the Provos, and that girl, had been loading into the van at the 'double stop' farm.

'The Tank's closed, and the canteen's closed, guv,' the sergeant responded.

'Obviously the Tank and the canteen's closed. The coffee machine on the second floor.'

'I happen to know, guv, that the coffee machine on the second floor's bust.'

Regan glared at the young sergeant as if he knew to whom to attribute the breaking of the coffee machine. Then he got up, picked up the empty Bank Raid file cover, put the photo in it, and headed for the door.

'Sir, if you're taking that photo, sir, could I have a signature for it?' The young sergeant suddenly and correctly official.

Regan halted, turned two cold blue eyes on the boy and let a silence fall and be felt. 'If the appropriate people had put their appropriate signatures on that file and assigned it to the appropriate department, I would not have spent two hours looking for it. I'm Inspector Regan, Flying Squad. This photo will be returned to C.O.C.9. records tomorrow morning. And you gather the rest of that crap up, and rush it to C.9 where it belongs. Now.'

Regan walked out.

He chose the Maze Coffee Bar of the Kensington Garden Hotel. With the Rover 3500 wrecked at the farm, Len was now driving a Consul Estate from the Flying Squad spare car pool. He turned it into the kerb and braked. 'How long, guv?'

'An hour, two hours. I don't know. You go home.'

He saw Len take the Consul pointing off down Kensington High Street, and walked down into the basement restaurant.

He looked at his watch. One forty-five am. He ordered eggs, bacon, brown hash and chips, coffee black, and a full pot of it. He'd been up twenty hours now. It wasn't the physical exhaustion that worried him. It was its effect on

159

his mental condition. The problems of the case were now ones that had to be worked out by brainpower. He knew, some intuitive feeling, that he'd done all the leg work necessary. Now it was down to shoving back the coffee, staying wide awake, alert, keeping the machinery of mind working flat out. He had to find the solution to a problem that Sergeant Carter, Haskins, Maynon didn't even know existed.

He had the photograph of the Letchworth fracas in the file on the table. He took it out, studied it again. Each individual item of the Westminster Bank blaggers' equipment lined along the white washed wall at the back of the bank. The thermic lance itself, rubber hose, oxygen and hydrogen bottles; huge bottles, as if they were going to cut through the safe, then cut the building in half as an encore. Two pairs of Tuf boots, three pairs of asbestos mittens. Two asbestos helmets with silicate visors. Two suits of protective clothing. Step-up transformer, manual cutters, electrical equipment for re-circuiting alarm systems, jemmies, a hydraulic ram for recalcitrant wooden doors or windows. That was about it.

On a previous occasion a significant move had been made in this case by crow-eyed Ewing of the Frisco Mounties noticing that a shirt worn by Declan Murray in a photo from the South of France would not have been sent home immediately after the photo session, to be laundered and stuck in a cupboard drawer; *ergo* the photo was old and misrepresented Declan Murray's presence in that country. Now at the 'Double Stop' farmhouse this morning, Regan had watched those poor bastards lug their thermic lance stuff out to the van. And there was something wrong there. Something odd, like what was happening to him this second in the Maze Coffee Bar in the Kensington Garden Hotel.

An adventure-seeking pouf was studying him. Regan's eyes came up hard and studied the pouf. The pouf misread an invitation. Regan was sitting on a bar stool. There were twenty people in the all-night café, mostly pastey-faced kids fresh from alfresco sex in Hyde Park, grass in their hair. Regan was the only one at a bar stool. The rest, including the adventuring pouf, at the tables. The pouf got up, approached, and sat down four stools from Regan. He noticed that Regan's and his own brand of cigarette coincided—Benson and Hedges. Regan had just tapped out one cigarette butt in the ashtray in front of him.

The pouf smiled on the coy side, and opened with an offering of his Benson and Hedges. 'Smokey?'

Regan looked at him expressionless. A deliberate, non-specific expression. 'Are you a homosexual?' he said quietly.

The pouf—he was about forty—gave a moment's flutter of eyelashes and imitation boyish smile. 'I am, if you are,' he said with a cheeky little toss of his shoulders.

'I'm not,' Regan said softly. He produced his wallet, opened it and showed his identity card. 'I'm a very aggressive policeman. And I'm giving you two minutes to pay your bill, plus VAT, plus ten per cent service, and fuck off. Or something appalling and original is going to happen to you.'

The pouf was already in retreat. He didn't wait for the bill, dropped a five-pound note on the table from which he'd approached. Then he was grabbing a silver-knobbed malacca walking-cane, a fur-collared black coat, and white gloves, and was off for the exit.

White gloves. Regan looked at the photograph. White

gloves. You cannot use thermic lance equipment without asbestos gloves. You cannot cut open steel bars, then cut through a safe without pulling away the off-cuts of white-hot metal, and you do that with asbestos gloves. Maybe three pairs of asbestos gloves: one for the cutter, the others for his mates. Regan remembered the procession of those lads from the farmhouse loading the van this morning. Every item of equipment corresponding to the Westminster Bank blaggers as per police photo. Except the gloves. He had seen no asbestos gloves. Why no gloves? It wasn't logical to conclude that they would keep every item of equipment at that farm, except the gloves which they'd keep elsewhere. No, he must come up with an answer for that one. And that other question. Ewing had expressed it first, but it had already been nagging on some nerve at the back of Regan's mind ever since the investigation started. Now it was coming forward and growing in significance: why import this very big draftsman just to bust a bank in London?

The Broker phoned Purcell at the Curzon House Hotel and spoke two sentences. 'Read the front page of the *Evening Standard*. I'll be with you in an hour.' He replaced the phone.

It was 10.40 pm. Purcell rang room service. 'Do you happens to have a copy of the *Evening Standard* left?'

They did.

An attractive little Spanish girl brought up the newspaper. Purcell looked at the front page and forgot about the attractive girl. She left the room without the tip of ten pence that he'd placed handily on the table.

TOP IRA MEN KILLED IN M4 CRASH. There was a photograph of a Ford Zodiac sliced in half by a nearside upright of a motorway bridge. Other debris from the car was spread across the road. Ambulance men and several police were in the photo.

Purcell rang room service again. He had been on the point of going to bed. He now ordered a pot of coffee.

The Broker turned up almost exactly an hour from his phone call. Purcell offered him the last cup of coffee in the pot.

'We've lost our leader, Declan Murray. And John Murphy and Joey O'Horgan.'

Purcell shrugged. 'So we jack it in, and fuck off?'

The Broker tried a sip of warm coffee. Purcell had a feeling the Broker was holding something back.

'Look, some of these lads, as you know, are just professional blaggers, have no connection with the IRA.'

'Out with it,' Purcell said softly.

'Look, it seems like you've done some good drafting work on this job. And now suddenly the man who was both our boss and a terrible frightening man has gone from us. . . .'

Purcell reached inside his jacket and pulled the Smith and Wesson from the shoulder holster in one movement and pointed it at the Broker's head. 'Lay it on the line,' he ordered.

The Broker shrugged. 'Okay. We held something back from you. On Declan Murray's instructions. There's a man called Ewing, an American, a Peeler, in London, looking for you. Declan sent two of his boys out after him. They disappeared. Nothing heard of them since.'

Purcell was quiet a moment, then said aloud, but really talking to himself: 'Could be a cop from back home. I ran into some trouble Stateside, Mr Kavanagh. They maybe sent someone across . . .'

'So what I'm saying is, I think Declan Murray should've told you.'

'You're not saying that at all. You're pissing around, stalling, while I stick a gun on you. And what you're not talking about is this job. I want to talk about it right now.'

He put the gun back in its holster. He knew Kavanagh was carrying a gun. He knew there was a high chance that after he made his proposition Kavanagh would go for his gun. Purcell reckoned he'd have his Smith and Wesson handed and fired first. 'See here, Mr Kavanagh,' he said it slowly, distinctly, as if he didn't want the Broker to miss a word, 'there's a job set up and ready to go. And it's a better looking job because the man we were to give the money to is dead. Now I've been working out something for the last hour since I read that newspaper. It goes like this. There's a better way to pull this heist than the way we've been discussing up to now. But it means definitely sacrificing limbs or lives. What d'you think?'

The Broker was quiet. Purcell took the silence for part approval. 'Let me tell you what we have to do, Mr Kavanagh. We have to find four guys, four new guys, urgently. Can that be done?'

The Broker was nodding.

'Now to the point. I've worked hard on this project, so have you. Fuck all these other people. I want half the proceeds. You can have the other half.'

Purcell was sitting on the edge of his seat, every muscle flexed and ready to go for his gun, as soon as the Broker dived for his. But the Broker sat back in his chair, nodding slowly.

Purcell was pleased. He'd found what he'd come to London to search for on this job—a partner.

Regan took his problems home with him, went to bed with them, in his mother's little room, lay awake with them, and watched the cold dawn come up over Hammersmith. And he slowly dismissed all the other problems that had dominated the hours before bed as he began to concentrate on the major problem, which was not really about some bank job, but about a person, himself. He had reached the crisis of his whole career. A crisis not about Ewing or asbestos gloves but about a certain ambitious young Sergeant, George Carter, a creature invented, educated and perfected by Jack Regan, who was out to finish him by grabbing his case. There were few plums around larger than the Purcell-Declan Murray connection. If Carter got away with it, within days the top brass would be saying: 'Sod that for a lark—Detective Inspector Regan's slipping. Sergeant Carter solved his case and if Carter's better than Regan, let's promote him to Regan's status. And who's selected to give Regan an efficiency-improving boot up the arse, and/or marching orders?'

It would be marching orders. Not because of anything that the brass at the Yard felt. It would be Regan's own decision to resign. For a simple reason. As long as he was getting results, he could bend the rules. He could say to the chiefs of Flying Squad who ran it as a team effort: 'Bugger your wonderful team. I'm on a disappearing trick. Next time you see me I'll have the evidence, and the villains under arrest.' He could only do that while he was on top of the heap. Now it looked as if Carter was going to shoulder him off. There was another element to be considered. Regan had made a lot of enemies in his years on the Squad. Enemies were not important until their enemy became vulnerable. Regan studied the dawn filtering on to the flat grey palette of London skyline. There are a lot of people around who'd like my balls, he thought. Many.

The bedside table drawer contained a life-support system. Bottle of fifty Dexedrin and a bottle of Mogadon. He took out the bottle of Mogadon, opened it, and took two.

It was true that the investigation had reached the stage now where all the phenomena needed to solve it were probably there, and despite nearly a day without sleep he should be at his desk at the Yard. On the other hand, despite the histrionics in Carter's and Ewing's report about 'immediate action' etcetera, there was no doubt that nothing was going to happen tonight at 300 Eastcheap because it was now four am in the morning. So it would not be happening tonight, Sunday night. Perhaps tomorrow night.

Regan, flat on his back in the big brass bed, mind starting to slow now, but annoyingly returning with a jerk each time he hit the point of sleep. It was that bastard report. Something wrong with it. Carter, aided and abetted in anonymity by Ewing, the kraut-baller and mick-breaker. Lieutenant Ewing, his remorseless quest for that unknown quantity, James Purcell. Purcell, America's Mr Big in the Planning Department, comes to London to knock over a bank. Doesn't sound right. Now, if he'd come to London to knock over a dozen banks . . .

Detective Inspector Jack Regan sat bolt upright in bed as if a steam-hammer had hit him in the stomach.

166

He did eventually get to sleep. About six o'clock Monday morning, to the tune of pigeons, starlings, and the chink of milk bottles on doorsteps. And muffled female screams from a newly married young couple two flats above who seemed to be on the job day and night. Regan approved of balling irrespective of race, creed, or time of day, provided neither party was a screamer. He loathed screaming birds, and blokes, and he'd landed a right coloratura two floors too near, and above.

When he'd realized what was wrong with Carter's report at four am, he'd pulled himself out of bed, made tea, put it down the sink because there was no milk, and made black coffee. Then he'd made notes.

The notes were incomprehensible except to him. But the last note, about the timing, was clear. There was no way it could happen on this overcast Monday morning with low clouds up there spoiling for rain. So there was no point in staying up any longer. He had popped another Mogadon, and smashed himself down on the bed, and gone to sleep immediately.

At seven am the phone rang. It was a sergeant assigned to Bomb Squad whose name he'd never heard, who gave him the news in a few brief sentences. Regan was so astounded that he asked the man to give the message again and slowly.

'I have been asked by Chief Inspector Patchin, officer in

charge of a combined Bomb Squad and Flying Squad operation, to inform you that a raid took place on the New York Bank and Trust Company at 300 Eastcheap two hours ago. The information we have is that there was a shoot-out and there are no survivors among the bank raiders. There have been two fatalities to policemen. Your presence is required at that address.' The young sergeant then asked if he required car and driver.

Regan told the sergeant to phone Len and tell him to meet his guvnor at the Eastcheap address. He put the phone down.

He threw back the bedcovers and sat for a moment on the edge of the bed. The news was totally beyond his comprehension.

A crowd of about three hundred had materialized on the damp streets of the City morning. Porters from large office blocks, night watchmen, workers from the Tubes and railway, and others, the occupants of City apartments who'd been shattered out of their sleep by the gunfire round the bank. Regan pulled his battered Jaguar up on to the low kerb at the west end of Eastcheap opposite the Tube Station, and about three hundred yards from the bank. As he climbed out of the car, he knew everything was wrong because of the double police cordon at the far end of the street.

He'd made one call to the switchboard sergeant at Squad —the only bloke who had probably heard, officially or unofficially, all the calls. Yes, the two security guards were abducted outside their office in South Audley Street, the police had followed the gang to Eastcheap, and the complete motorized operation of a hundred police had been on the spot within eight minutes. Regan strode across the first police cordon. The police only organized two cordons in an incident like this if they wanted to keep the press and others of the curious well away.

The first cordon, set up about fifty yards from the bank and in a semicircle around it, consisted of about eighty of the Special Patrol, all armed and glowering at the crowd which was still gathering in an odd kind of festive mood on the two pavements of the street. Regan went to the nearest Special Patrolman and identified himself. The man waved him away. Regan started forward. The man shouted at him sharply and gestured him back.

Regan unleashed a stream of invective telling the man in no uncertain terms that he was a policeman. The copper demanded identification. Probably for the only time in his life, Regan had none. He had left the apartment in a hurry, without his wallet. He made his way furiously down the outside of the police column which blocked the street.

He spotted Carter. Carter saw him and waved him through the first line of policemen.

'What's happened?'

'A mess. Two of our lot killed.'

'What about Purcell? The Provos?'

Carter shrugged and muttered something which Regan didn't catch because of the noise of two ambulances' bells clanging, arriving in the street simultaneously. Carter headed off to intercept the ambulances.

Regan strode on and through the second line of regular police and in through the wide doors of the bank.

There were fifty people inside. Maynon, Patchin, Flying Squad men, Bomb Squad men, some heavyweight Yard brass, the sort that came out of the woodwork whenever a police officer got killed, doctors, sharpshooters, ambulance men, police photographers, the ashen-faced bank Vice President Mr Harben, other bank personnel, all swelling voices and movements back and forth across the marbled floor smeared with blood and spent shells. The two dead policemen had been laid out on stretchers with their faces covered by newspapers. The others lay where they had fallen.

They were all dead, the IRA Provos. Regan walked slowly from one body to the other, ticking off their faces against the photographs appended to Carter's report.

Nobody, none of the high, confused and histrionic voices of the mob in the bank spoke to him. He continued the round of dead bodies. The brothers, Tim and Tony Noonan, lay within a yard of each other on the floor on the inside of the bank counter. Tom George Martin, the SNP bloke, had been cut down on the marble stairs leading down to the bank vaults. Traynor, who looked as if he was about fifteen years of age, propped in a window ledge, a Colt automatic at his feet. The window had been blown out by the same blast of firing that had almost cut the boy's body in half.

Regan's eyes left the bodies and looked uncomprehendingly into the faces of the babbling police and officials. How could it have happened? How could these people have conspired in their madness to manufacture such a slaughter? How was it possible? All dead. Not one arrest. A massacre.

He stumbled on, and found the body of Cathy Traynor, her throat and chest ripped open by heavy-calibre fire. He went down the stairs into the vaults. They hadn't even had the chance to assemble their thermic lance equipment before the gun battle began. More bodies. One propped face to the wall. He turned it over, to check the identity, breaking the most important rule in the book: photographers first before a body is moved. But he didn't care about rules any more.

He straightened up. The idiots upstairs babbling and shouting. Carter, Maynon, Haskins babbling. What the fuck were they talking about, why the hell were they blundering around here when the three people who really mattered were missing? Where was Lieutenant Ewing? Where was the one they called the Broker? Where was Purcell? Regan knew. And Regan also knew that Maynon, Haskins and bird-brain Carter didn't, had no idea that this whole thing was a plant, a set-up. Ewing had once said it, he was going to set himself up as a clay-pigeon. This was a diversion. The real birds had flown to the real addresses.

He stepped slowly up the stairs and walked, almost staggered, out of the bank.

Nausea hit him. He'd seen death many times before. It wasn't the general slaughter, or the particular execution of the girl, it was the pointlessness of it—the fact that Patchin, Maynon, all of them had been conned. Conned into a bloody massacre. That was hard to take. He staggered along, still steeped in Mogadon. He'd had exactly one hour's sleep.

The cold air of the City hit into him. Someone was speaking to him as his stride hit the fresh grit of the street surface. It was Carter, asking him questions, giving him explanations—which were all now unanswerable and beyond relevance. He pushed through the first line of policemen. Carter kept after him, gripped his sleeve. Regan stopped, shouted some obscenities close into the sergeant's face. He saw Carter back off, surprised. But then Regan was moving again, through the second line of police, through the crowd behind it, who shouted more questions at him—they'd seen him come out of the bank. He put a hand up to fend off their queries and their voices. Then he broke into a trot, he felt his gut begin to heave. But he made it to Len in the Consul without being sick.

'Len, don't say anything, turn off the engine. Listen to me. Just let me talk. That fuck-up over the road, a diversion. The IRA imported the best draftsman in the world, not to plan a heist on that American bank in London, but to rob all of them. Except that one. To rob every American bank that shared the same security system, in one fast operation. They have in common a security system which operates a timing device for opening their safes at nine am every morning. . . .'

Len started a slow head shake to protest he wasn't following. But Regan was really talking to himself. 'The time now is seven twenty-five. The time on the clock above the safe in that bank over there reads ten-fifteen. In other words, an hour and a quarter ago it would have been possible to open the bank safe without thermic lances or anything, if you knew the combination.'

Len now elevating his eyes to the ceiling of the car, not understanding a word. 'I don't get this, guv.'

Regan's eyes still on the street, still studying the chaos of police and ambulances around the bank. 'What's important is that I understood it at six o'clock this morning, though I didn't realize they could get at the time mechanism of the clock. I think Lieutenant Ewing understood that earlier.' He handed a yellow page to Len. 'I ripped this out of Yellow Pages (Central). It's a list of banks. I've underlined all those I think are American. Len, we have to get round those addresses faster than you've ever driven a car before. Understand?'

Len nodded.

'Right. First one, Anglo-American Interbank, Cornwallis Street.'

Len touched the starter. The engine kicked over and roared. Len slipped the revs to four thousand and let in the

172

clutch. A hundred policemen and three hundred spectators watched the Consul, rear-deck down, burn black lines of tyre prints down Eastcheap and slew round the west corner of the road heading deeper into the City.

'Squad 501, Squad 501,' Regan calling MP at Scotland Yard, shouting into the head-set which he held against the door of the screaming, yawing car, his other hand jammed against the facia, as also his knees.

'Squad 501, receiving,' the Radio Room at the Yard came back.

'Squad 501, our car registration Hotel Juliet, Juliet fifty-one L, Lima, proceeding over limit to various addresses City of London. For reasons of surprise approach, we will not be using Winkworth gong. Inform City police patrols we are in this area and not to intercept, message timed 0730 hours, over.'

'Squad 501, we have message for officer in charge to report immediately to his superior officer at CO, repeat immediately and urgently, MP over.'

Regan wound down the window of the car, which was now hitting ninety on City Road, and stuck the hand-mike out into the air flow. That would sound like bad static back at MP. Then he pulled the mike half-way in and shouted at it. 'Squad 501, please repeat. Reception poor, try another channel, over. . . .'

Regan stuck the hand-mike back, wound up the window, looked at Len's white face, hazel eyes boring into the thin line trickle of early morning traffic, trying to work out the equation between tyre adhesion, brakes, and the moves of fellow car travellers in the dazed perspective of their early morning driving. MP blathered on, uncertainly calling for Squad 501, but eventually concluding an R/T fault, or the car travelling in some freak reception area. Regan was not reporting to any senior officer. He was now on his own.

Len pulled the car screaming off Fenchurch Street and burned a path in rubber smoke on a right-hander north up Cullun Street and into Lime Street, heading for their third American bank. Like the first two banks they'd covered, they'd evolved a system. The instant Len braked, Regan was out of the car, testing the bank's front door, looking in the windows. Or, as in the case of the first bank, where the glass was frosted to ten feet above ground, Len pushed the car up on to the pavement and Regan climbed on the car's roof.

At the New Boston Chartered Bank, Lime Street, Regan slammed out of the car and himself skidded to a halt. The front door of the bank was wide open, like some security man's nightmare. Although he approached carefully, he was finally in and out of the bank in less than two minutes. Not a soul inside. The main safe at the back of the building wide open, and cleaned out.

Regan was hardly into the car when the tyres were burning off again. Len took a second's look at the next address in the ripped yellow sheet.

'Where?' Regan barked.

'Finch Lane, off Cornhill.'

'Are you sure we're motoring the shortest route between these banks?'

Len's eyes came off the road for one glance at him, ice cold. 'Finch Lane is one way south to north, sir,' Len said hard.

'Sorry,' Regan realized it was probably the first time in their years of working together that he'd ever had to apologize to Len. He felt it would not be the only historic landmark of this day.

174

Finch Lane was a developer's afterthought which happened during a stroll down Cornhill EC2 by a couple of Victorian hustlers who spotted, some time in the final decade of the last century, that families were moving out of Cornhill to be replaced by office edifices. And that the fine little mews lane where servants lived and loved in damp decrepitude could be flattened, and a red brick phoenix arise. Tall offices and higher rents. But it was not the Victorian architecture that interested Regan as Len slewed the car in a protesting lurch and then a skidding halt into Finch Lane. It was the sight of a half dozen SECURCOM vans, four of which were parked sideways, blocking the street at each end. From inside the building of the City American Bank of London, half-way up Finch Lane, came the sound of gunfire.

As Len slammed on the brakes, Regan's head nearly went through the windscreen. Then he was out and running past the first two vans that blocked the south exit of the street. In his hand he held the Smith and Wesson .38.

He saw a SECURCOM bloke armed with a truncheon who seemed to have more gold braid than any of the others. Regan headed for him. 'Detective Inspector Regan, Flying Squad. How many in there?'

The gold braid looked relieved by Regan's arrival. 'Three blokes, inside, down below.'

'What happened?'

The gold braid started to explain. There had been six altogether, four had escaped.

'So who's in there?'

'Mr Ewing and two of the gang, armed. I think one may be dead.'

'How did the other four escape? Is the rear of the building covered?'

'There's no way out. Rear of the bank is a solid wall.'

'What the fuck happened?'

'We were here first.' The SECURCOM man said it carefully as if there'd been so much confusion he had difficulty in recalling what happened. 'Mr Ewing didn't expect so many. There were six, plus the two kidnapped security guys.'

'What happened to them?'

'When the shooting started they ran off.'

'When did all this happen?'

'Three minutes ago.'

'Jesus, why didn't you say! So it's Ewing and two robbers in there?'

The security man nodded.

Regan missed the nod. He ran on, hit the front porch of the bank, and threw himself in and down.

There was a man lying a yard away from him, his hair entirely soaked in blood, as if a tin of red paint had been emptied over him. Only his eyes clear of blood, and open, staring at Regan. The name on Carter's report under the photo of this man had been James Kavanagh—nickname, the Broker. The Broker was dead.

No one else in sight in the main bank hall.

The gunfire started again below. Regan looked around. The vault and the safe were approached by stairs at the back of the hall.

The gold-braided guy from SECURCOM was approaching Regan's rear, worming himself flat out across the carpet from the front door. 'Are there more Force on the way, sir?'

A burst of semi-automatic gunfire ricochetting off the walls below prevented Regan replying for a second.

'No. Get my driver to call MP,' Regan shouted at him. 'Tell him to get the Special Patrol Group here. Move!'

176

Regan started forward, working his body along on his elbows.

The SECURCOM man retreated quickly.

Regan reached the top of the stairs, brought his eyeline just over the top stair, and looked down.

It was a short flight, ten steps. At the bottom an open area and again the same set-up as in the New York Bank and Trust Company, Eastcheap. The steel-bar wall with the door set in it, wide open. The huge safe beyond it, its door slightly ajar. Probably open about twelve inches.

Regan's first glance also took in the geography left and right of the bottom of the stairs. He could work it out from the way the strip of brown carpet went down the stairs and met another strip which had further strips sewn to it, suggesting two carpeted corridors going back from the steel-bar fence.

Still on his stomach, he slid back a few feet into what he considered to be dead ground, safe from gunfire below. He cupped his hands to project his voice. 'Ewing, you down there?'

A long pause before the American's voice came back, as if he had been considering not answering. 'I'm here. Purcell's inside the safe. He has a pistol, and what looks like an FN 303. I'm stuck back of the left-hand corridor. He has the drop on me from behind the safe. He's protected by the safe door. You see it?'

Regan didn't answer for the moment. He was concentrating on the alternatives. He edged himself forward once more to raise his head slightly over the top of the stairs. He saw the safe door. He saw the tips of the fingers of Purcell's right hand come out from behind the edge of the door holding a lid broken off from a tin box—the kind of tin box that held Webley ammunition. Purcell was using the tin lid as a primitive mirror to spot the vaguest shadows on the stairs or in the corridor. Regan made a quick calculation that the safe was probably about eight feet square inside. Regan misjudged Purcell, the man he'd never met. The polished tin lid caught the three inches of the top of Regan's head emerging above the steps. The polished tin lid disappeared and the hand that had held it suddenly reappeared with a Biretta 380 automatic pistol and thumped off five shells up at Regan.

Regan jerked fast backwards. He cupped his hands again. 'Ewing, hear me?'

A muffled voice from below. 'Yes!'

'There may be a way to get this man out of the safe.'

The hand and the Biretta came out from behind the safe door to loose off four more shots. Regan felt the brush of air as they sailed past, a foot above his head, to thud into the ceiling plaster. 'The way I see it, Purcell has to keep the safe door open enough to be able to traverse his gun if you make a move. If he opens it too wide we've got him. But he must have it open nine inches at least to cover us.'

A pause. Then Ewing's voice. 'So?'

Regan manoeuvred himself over to the left-hand side of the staircase. He was going to attempt something definitely a little too ambitious for a gun not built for sharpshooting. He was going to fire off two or three shots rapidly down the stairs and try and get one through the gap of the open safe door and the doorframe. From his line of fire the gap was about three inches wide.

Purcell's two fingers holding the reflecting tin lid eased out from behind the door and checked the reflections of Regan and Ewing's areas. Regan from his recumbent position raised his left hand. The tin quickly disappeared. This was the moment before the hand with the Biretta would

178

reappear to fire the shots. Regan's body jerked up, right arm out, three rapid shots at the aperture, two wide, one dead centre about a foot above Purcell's hand, which now reappeared with the Biretta and then hastily withdrew.

And Regan knew why that hand withdrew. Because he could hear the fast thumps of six ricochets of the slug that got into the safe, as it slammed from one steel wall to another.

There was no scream from Purcell. The ricochetting bullet inside the safe in its half-dozen rebounds had somehow managed not to hit him. But Regan could imagine what Purcell was thinking. 'You get it, Purcell?' Purcell's hand had not reappeared with the Biretta. 'If you close the door of the safe you're finished and trapped. If you open it a bit more to get a bead on me or Ewing, you're also in trouble. I'm going to lie here potting shells in through that gap, and one of them, on its ricochetting path is going to hit you. The odds are in my favour, right?'

The odds were not all in Regan's favour, as he had learned a second ago. One of the bullets that hadn't got through the aperture had hit the steel door and ricochetted back up the stairway to pass within a yard of his head. There was a distinct chance in calculating the angles that he might intercept his own ricochet off the safe door, up the stairs. He decided he'd take the risk.

He allowed a minute's silence, jerked up fast again, loosed off another two shots. Again one of them got through the gap, and he could hear it bouncing from wall to wall and then a sharp scream that lasted a second. Then silence. But no sound of any body falling over.

'Purcell, are you coming out?' Regan asked matter of factly.

A long pause from below. Regan wondering why Ewing

was saying nothing. He took out a clip and started to re-load the Smith and Wesson. 'You want more? Fine. Your choice.' He wondered if Purcell believed him. He, Regan didn't mean it. This man he wanted alive to go on trial. He wanted Purcell on trial, so that Patchin, Maynon, Carter and the others would have to explain in a court their part in pointless, panic slaughter at 300 Eastcheap.

Then suddenly the voice below said low and hard: 'Okay, you shits, I'm coming out.'

'First your guns. Throw them,' Regan commanded.

'Of course, of course,' Purcell said, as if he'd heard that specific order a thousand times before and was getting bored with it.

The Biretta hit and bounced across the floor. Then the FN 303 was thrown out and the door of the safe pushed open. Regan stood up levelling his gun at Purcell. Ewing strolled into view below. Suddenly, as if by some sixth sense, SECURCOM men were milling into the bank. The one Regan had spoken to was saying something about an un-specified police car that had appeared outside.

Purcell stood there. The ricochet had sliced across the back of his left hand. The wound was bleeding on to the floor but the man didn't seem to care.

Regan looked from the first American to the other, to Ewing. Ewing standing there, eyes slowly going up and down Purcell, working on some calculation. Was this the time to tell this other American, the cop, that he too was under arrest? Because Regan was going to nail him, was going to arrest him at some point, off his own bat, for the bloody assault and calculated torture of Declan Murray. But no, this was not the time. But the time would be soon enough.

Regan gestured with his gun. Purcell slowly headed up

the carpeted stairs. The two cops headed after him. Regan's expression was inscrutable.

They went out through the confused and bewildered SECURCOM lot into the street. Ewing took Regan's arm. 'I don't want to hang around. I don't want to get mixed up with Maynon, Carter. I want some answers before they get their hands on this man. Do me a favour. Leave your driver here to deal with these cops. You, me, Purcell go in my car to an interview room in your nearest police station. Right?'

Regan was already nodding, agreeing. He also wanted Purcell and Ewing alone, just the three of them in an interview room somewhere where he could get straight answers to some complicated questions. He paced over to Len, gave him a twenty-second rundown on what had happened, told him to wait for Maynon, Haskins and the others, and deal with a uniformed traffic patrol which had arrived and had exchanged words with the SECURCOM people and was now approaching Regan. Regan nodded to the two cops. 'Detective Inspector Regan. He'll tell you.' He thumbed towards Len. Then he crossed the road to where Ewing was leading Purcell to the hired Jaguar.

'Would you drive?' Ewing asked.

Regan got into the driver's seat. Ewing indicated for Purcell to get in the back, then he got in the front of the car with Regan. But he sat sideways in the seat, his big Navy Colt covering Purcell through the gap between the front seats.

Regan accelerated the car forward. 'We can go to West End Central, Cannon Row, or maybe Bow Street is nearer and . . .'

'Anywhere,' Ewing said quietly.

Ten seconds later the car was screaming up Leadenhall

181

Street heading for Aldgate. Ewing suddenly ordered, 'Turn right here.' He was pointing to the narrow opening of Mitre Street.

'Why?' Regan asked, puzzled. He had understood the route was his province.

'Don't argue. Turn. I'll explain.' Ewing's voice had an urgency in it.

Regan didn't question further, lurched the car over right, and headed into the side street. There was no movement, traffic or people in the little street. Not one single person, male or female, in the tiny street at that hour in the morning. And that was what Ewing was searching for. An empty street with no witnesses.

'Brake. Stop the car,' Ewing ordered.

'Why?' Regan, annoyed and puzzled, barked the question back. But he touched the brakes and the car slowed down slightly and steadied.

Ewing lifted the Navy Colt .45 containing his last dumdum bullet, and pointed it straight at the forehead of James Purcell, and blew most of his head off.

They sat and faced each other in Maynon's office—Maynon, Haskins, and Regan. Regan had entered the office twenty seconds ago. Maynon had waved him to a seat. Regan had sat and waited whilst Maynon got the tobacco into his pipe.

Outside not a sound in the corridor, not even the tap of the Squad secretaries' typewriters. Out there, sixty to seventy detectives and other personnel knew that something important was happening in the Guvnor's office. And they knew positively that it was not going to be a meeting of words, but a collision.

It took Maynon a long time and a number of matches to get his pipe alight. The worrying thing from Regan's point of view was that Haskins was saying nothing. At last Maynon looked up and spoke softly. 'You're a stupid bastard.' He shook his head slowly from side to side. He looked at Haskins. 'Show him.'

Haskins pulled out his wallet and took the typed note out as if it was his own private property instead of an official Scotland Yard Inter Office Memo. He handed it to Regan.

Regan read it, shrugged, handed it back.

'That's it in a nutshell. Within three days of Ewing arriving in England, Carter sent that memo to Haskins. Haskins didn't act on it. That's not the point. The milk's spilt. We expect, with your co-operation,' Maynon said it as if it was an element that was naturally to be relied on, 'with your co-operation, we sweep the lot under the carpet.'

'I'm not following you, sir,' Regan replied quietly.

'I'm saying two things. Sergeant Carter had a quiet think about Lieutenant Ewing and did some discreet investigating. He found out that, although Ewing had been in England three days, he had made no move whatsoever to set in train with the Home Office the organizing of extradition papers for the man he intended to arrest. When Carter found out that Ewing wasn't here to locate and extradite Purcell to the US, he came to the inevitable conclusion. Ewing was here on a vengeance mission. He was here to execute the police-killer Purcell.'

'Now he goes to jail for it,' Regan said softly.

'That's not my point. My point is, why did Carter think of doing a check on Ewing, and not you?'

Regan glared at Maynon. 'What would you like me to say, sir? That fortunate we are indeed to have amongst us this gift of God, Sergeant Carter?'

'I'm saying, Regan, you're not a very bright copper.'

183

Regan, his eyes hard on Maynon's, allowed a grim silence to tick on for a full half a minute.

And still Haskins said nothing.

Regan suddenly gave a shrug, as if he'd dismissed the whole thing from his mind. 'All right, what are we going to do about this murdering bastard Ewing?' he said matter of factly.

Maynon looked at Haskins as if he expected Haskins to give the news, and Haskins began to open his mouth, and for some reason Maynon raised his hand. Maynon had elected to take the responsibility. He put the tips of his fingers together and faced Regan. 'It's a question of whose story to believe. Three people in the car, one dead. You were driving. Lieutenant Ewing's story is that he told you to stop the car. He wanted to interrogate Purcell in the car, try to get an admission about the killing of O'Hagen before the whole of London CID descended on Purcell, the bank robber. He told you to stop the car. You banged on the brakes. The car lurched. An accident. The gun went off. That's his story.'

'It's a fucking lie.'

'Your story,' Maynon said it as if it was a question of simple choice. 'I believe Lieutenant Ewing is a very, very experienced police officer. I don't think he'd have any problems convincing a coroner of his accident story. I don't see any future in the two of you going into a lengthy court case and calling each other liars. Furthermore, I do not believe that the Director of Public Prosecutions would in this . . .'

Regan got up and walked out of the office.

The concourse of Terminal Three, Oceanic, London Airport, has its exits and its entrances. To the Swiftian observer noting the large numbers entering by foot and leaving on wings, Spring through Summer, it would appear a matter of months before the entire population be drained forever from this British island. And not within distance of easy return. These people have chosen Oceanic. Not the other two buildings, the cross country, or European terminals. These travellers want to put oceans between themselves and the sinking, bankrupt island. Not channels, nor mere continents, oceans. They want out, far and fast. The travel office at New Scotland Yard had told Regan a booking had been made for Ewing on Pan Am Polar 102 back to San Francisco. Flight time, midday. Boarding time, eleven-thirty. Regan pushed open the swing doors on the ground floor of Terminal Three and was confronted by a sea of humanity. He had possibly seconds to find Ewing before he got on the plane. He took the escalator directly on his left to the first floor. It was eleven-thirty.

At the far end of the first floor passport formalities and the walkway to the planes. And on the floor itself about two thousand people.

Regan strode across the Pirelli flooring. Some people got in his way, he pushed them aside. Others saw his expression, and moved aside. And although Ewing should already be heading towards the Passport Officers, he hadn't made the move, and Regan spotted him just for one fraction of a second in a small gap in the seething crowd.

Ewing was standing, back to him, window shopping in the huddle of kiosks selling Pringle sweaters, tartan kilts, and Yardley perfume.

He paced in on Ewing. Len's hundred-mile-an-hour drive up the motorway, Winkworth gong blasting, had got Regan here with perhaps just a few seconds to spare.

That's all Regan required—a few seconds. He approached the back of Lieutenant Ewing and tapped him on the shoulder.

Ewing turned.

Regan brought his right hand back, bunched hard, and hit the American a crippling punch just below the heart.

Ewing's lungs exploded air in Regan's face. Ewing stepped back and sank to his knees.

Regan turned. At the same deliberate pace that he'd approached Ewing, he walked away from him, ignoring the witnesses who'd seen that punch, and the big man go down, witnesses frozen to the spot with amazement and disbelief.

Regan didn't know where he was heading. Then he did know. He could see just to the left of the escalators, the bar. It was open. He headed over to it. A scotch, and then on with life as it is lived.

There were four customers at the bar, ranged along its length like permanent extensions of the bar stools. Not travellers, probably off-duty porters, or taximen, none with baggage.

Regan formulated the immediate plan. A large scotch, which he ordered. Then Len to drive him home. Then a call to the Yard to say he was taking the day off at their convenience, or inconvenience. Then he'd open a bottle of Teacher's, and drink most of it, and work it out. Whether to stick with this lousy job, or jack it in immediately. And he wondered how he already knew that the decision would be to stick with the fucking job.

There was a tap on Regan's shoulder.

Regan swung round on Ewing.

'What d'you want?' Regan demanded, his fists bunched and ready. Ewing studied him, shrugged, sat down two bar stools away, caught the barman's eye. 'Do you have Jim Beam?'

The barman nodded.

'A small Jim Beam.'

The barman poured, came over, put the drink down. Ewing spun a fifty-pence piece with a flick of his wrist. The barman picked up the spinning coin.

Regan's eyes down on his own drink. 'You'll miss your bloody plane.'

'I've checked in. They know I'm here, they'll wait a bit,' Ewing said. 'Jesus, you throw a mean right. . . .'

Regan turned, looked at him. 'What d'you want?'

The American shrugged again. 'I would like to buy you a drink, Jack Regan.'

Regan looked him over slowly, closely, as if it was the moment for a final conclusion about Ewing, a conclusion to file away permanently in his own mind, for his own purposes. 'No,' he said gently, almost wearily. 'I don't want a drink from you.'

Ewing was studying Regan, calculating some kind of equation whereby he could leave this strange English cop, not quite one hundred per cent hating him.

Regan made it difficult for him, or perhaps easy. He got up, and walked off.

Ewing listened to the third public address call for Flight 102, swallowed down his drink, and headed away towards Passport Control and the walkway to the planes.

4